# REMY AND THE SEX ALIENS

RILEY ROSE

BOOK ONE IN THE REMY AND THE SEX MONSTERS SERIES

Cover Design by Kingofdesigner on Fiverr



Originally published on Kindle Vella as Remy and the Sex Monsters: Episodes 1-15.

Read all the Episodes of Remy and the Sex Monsters on Kindle Vella

Sign-Up for my E-Mail List to Stay Up-To-Date on New Releases!

Visit RileyRoseErotica.com for more sexy stories!

# Chapter 1

Remy Alvarez walked out of the Mystery Marquee movie theater, stretching her arms over her head, which thrust out her impressive tits. They weren't ridiculously huge, but they were firm and bouncy and contained nipples that always poked out underneath her T-shirts. She was wearing a red one at the moment, along with cut-off jean shorts, revealing her long, tan legs. Her shorts barely contained her curvy, juicy booty, a booty that attracted plenty of attention wherever she went.

She flung her long, brunette locks behind her as she turned to her friends. "Wasn't that awesome?" she asked gleefully.

"It was awesome catching up on sleep," Ryan replied, scratching the beard he was trying to grow.

"The popcorn was good," Lily added.

Remy flung her arms down, which made her boobs bounce again. "Aw, c'mon guys. That was the greatest sci-fi movie marathon ever!"

Ryan rolled his eyes. "Maybe the corniest movie marathon ever."

Remy hopped up and down, which, of course, meant more boob bouncing. She wasn't trying to bounce them. She just got uber-excited about anything sci-fi or paranormal. "But that's what makes them so great!"

Lily patted Ryan's shoulder. "You know our girl loves bad B-movies."

"Yup, she's a weirdo."

Remy stuck her tongue out at him. "You guys just don't understand great cinema."

Lily wrapped her arms around Remy's waist and kissed her on the cheek. "We understand we love hanging out with you."

Remy beamed and smothered them both in a hug. "Aw, you guys are the best!"

"Want a ride home?" her pretty, blonde-haired friend asked.

"No thanks, it's so nice out, I'll just walk.

"I bet you hope you'll run into aliens on the way home," Ryan teased.

That led to more excited boob-shaking. "How cool would

that be!"

Lily gave her another hug. "Well, text me later and tell me what the aliens are like."

Remy saluted. "You got it!"

Her friends laughed and headed for Ryan's car.

Remy snapped a selfie in front of the brightly lit marquee, then shoved the phone in her back pocket. While her friends might not appreciate classic cinema, she was thrilled the old movie theater still operated in her small town. They played stuff you couldn't find anywhere else, not even on the seemingly hundreds of streaming services available. And it was run by a guy who knew everything about every bad sci-fi movie ever made. And by bad, she meant amazing! The owner, Mr. Jenkins, was even kind enough to let her into the projection booth from time to time and show her the old reels. So cool!

She took a shortcut through Old Man Smithers's field. He'd yell at her in his adorably cranky way if he spotted her, like he had for the past twenty years, but he'd be long asleep. It was 2:00 a.m. and all she could hear were the crickets chirping.

She gazed up at the starry sky. One good thing about

living in a small town was little to no light pollution, which gave spectacular views of the heavens.

She was so lost in her stargazing, she smacked right into something hard.

"Ow!" she yelped, falling backward on her butt.

She looked up but there was nothing in front of her. What the heck?

She got to her feet and put her hands out gingerly. They landed on a cool, metallic surface. She snatched them back, shocked by the invisible object in front of her.

She tentatively stepped forward again, feeling more of the mysterious machine. Whatever it was, it was big. She circled around at least thirty yards without coming to the end.

Eventually, she felt a groove in the smoothness and then heard a click.

An entry ramp lowered with a whoosh. A brilliant bright light illuminated Remy and the field.

She stood there in shock. This couldn't really be happening. Was she still in the theater, the dozen hours of movies invading her dreams? Or was she really standing before an alien spaceship?

She knew the smart thing to do would be to run away as

fast as she could. But there was no way she could give up on an opportunity to see the inside of an alien spacecraft. This was literally her dream come true!

She walked slowly up the ramp, shielding her eyes from the intense light.

When she got to the top, it was much dimmer. The interior was a cool, metallic gray. Everything was smooth and polished. It definitely looked like how she envisioned an alien ship.

But what really confirmed it were the five aliens adjusting control panels that looked straight out of the movies.

The aliens were a lighter gray then the ship. They had small bodies and large, oblong heads. They looked very much like the drawings from all the abduction tales.

Remy couldn't believe it. She still didn't know if she was dreaming.

But then all five of the creatures looked at her. And it felt way more real.

They stared with unblinking eyes.

Remy was frozen. She didn't know if she should make a run for it or make first contact. What would Captain Pike from Star Trek do?

She waved awkwardly. "Um, hi. Welcome to Earth." She wanted to facepalm. That was such a lame greeting. She should have said something super-cool and profound. What the heck were all those years of watching science-fiction good for if they didn't teach her how to welcome aliens to the planet?

They remained staring at her. Until one of them took out a small device.

"Um, that's not a laser..." Her question was cut off as an energy beam streaked across the room and hit her in the chest.

*Yup, it was a laser gun,* she thought just before she lost consciousness.

***

She opened her eyes slowly. She tried to move her limbs but couldn't. She thought it might be an effect of the laser blast, but then realized she was strapped to a table.

Her eyes opened much wider. She was on her back on a rectangular exam table, the same color as the rest of the ship. Her wrists were clasped in metallic restraints above her and her ankles in similar ones, except they were fastened so her legs were spread.

And she was completely naked.

*Oh. Shit.* All the stories of alien probing were true. Captain Pike never had to deal with this!

Her nipples stuck upward, even harder than they usually were due to the coolness of the ship's interior. Her pussy lips glistened under the light that illuminated only her. She liked to keep it shaved in case, well, a situation like this ever happened. She had fantasized about this scenario many times, but never thought it would come true.

The five aliens stepped out of the darkness and surrounded the table, peering down at her naked body.

Remy squirmed under their scrutiny. She was blessed with the best traits from her French mother and Mexican father, so most people found her quite sexy. But she didn't know what aliens liked. Apparently they were into BDSM since she was tied up. Remy had always wanted to experiment with bondage. She just didn't think her first time would be with aliens.

"Um, do you guys like Earth girls?" she asked. Ugh, that was another dumb question. But they weren't talking, so she felt she needed to fill the silence. And she always liked being friendly to new people she met: humans or aliens.

In response, one of them pressed a button on a control panel next to the bed and a huge phallic object rose out of a secret panel between Remy's legs.

Her eyes got huge. Though not nearly as huge as the silver dildo-looking device that was inching toward her lips.

Holy shit. She was about to get pussy probed by aliens.

# Chapter 2

"Is this what you guys do on all your first dates?" Remy asked, her eyes locked on the pussy probe closing in on her lips.

The five gray-skinned aliens didn't respond. Their gazes were focused on her wettening mound. Oh geez, she hadn't realized she had gotten so wet. She should probably be freaking out, but the idea of a bunch of aliens watching her be probed by their huge device was very exciting, if a little embarrassing.

"Am I the first human girl you've met?" She knew they likely couldn't understand her. But she talked a lot when she got nervous. And it was eerily silent inside the ship. The only sounds were the faint hum of their alien craft and the mechanized shaft propelling the dildo-probe forward.

That probe touched her lips, parting them slightly.

She gasped, her nipples getting even harder.

The aliens glanced at each other, seemingly to

communicate in some unspoken language. Or maybe they were speaking telepathically. That'd be so cool. Almost as cool as how the probe felt against her lips.

It spread them further, penetrating her barrier.

"Ohhhhhh!" she moaned. "Fuck, that's big!"

The aliens made gestures to each other. They seemed to be making note of all her reactions. Was this experiment to see how human females reacted to sexual stimulation? If so, Remy felt it was her duty to participate. Her cooperation could mean the difference between peace and war between Earth and these aliens.

"Could you stick it in a little more, please?" Besides wanting intergalactic peace, she really wanted to be fucked. Being naked, bound, ogled, and penetrated had made her one horny girl.

The probe burrowed farther into her. She squirmed on the table. She hadn't had anything this large inside her before. She wondered if they'd let her take the dildo home. Actually, were they going to let her go home? Surely they would after they finished probing her. Right? Remy didn't have time to think about that. The silver cock had completely filled her, brushing up against her cervix.

She whimpered on the table, her hips wiggling around as she tried to adjust to the alien behemoth.

That led to a lot more mental notes by the aliens. Their looks and gestures became more rapid. She didn't know how to read aliens, but they seemed to be getting more excited.

"You like seeing my pussy stuffed?" she asked coyly. Oh God, was she flirting with them? Would they take that as a sign she wanted to be their alien slut?

The device began vibrating inside her.

"Oh fuck, I'm an alien slut!" Her hips bucked off the table, the sensations making her lose control. Well, it certainly didn't take long for her to totally give in to them. But if she was going to be a slut for anyone, it might as well be aliens. Maybe they'd make her wear the Princess Leia slave girl outfit and take her around the galaxy, fucking her on a variety of wondrous planets. Okay, maybe she was getting carried away. But it was hard not to with voyeuristic aliens gazing at her writhing, nude body.

The vibrating device plunged in and out of her, filling her to capacity every time.

Her moans filled the sterile cabin. Her pussy got wetter with every thrust. She was completely helpless, and she fucking loved it!

"Please fuck me harder!" she begged.

They did. The dildo slammed into her, vibrating at speeds none of her sex toys could achieve.

"Ohhhh my fuccckkkiiiing Goddddddddd!" She screamed, flailing on the table. She had lost control of her body. The restraints were the only thing keeping her from doing more intense sexual gymnastics.

That familiar feeling welled up in her. But more intense than she had ever experienced.

"Oh fuck, I'm going to cum!!" She exploded, her entire body wracked by the most intense orgasm of her life. In fact, she even squirted. Wait, what? She was squirting? Holy shit, she had never done that before. But there were multiple streams of cum shooting out every which way around the probe.

She was proud of her newfound sexual ability. She couldn't wait to tell Lily about it. Though she might leave out the part about aliens, so her friend didn't think she was an even bigger weirdo than usual.

Her squirting ability make the aliens' eyes expand. She didn't know that was possible with how huge their orbs already were. They peered down at her non-stop gushing pussy.

Remy would have turned beet red at five aliens examining her squirt gun, but she was too busy shrieking in utter bliss.

When the probe finally eased out of her, her hips and thighs were drenched. And there was a huge pool of cum between her legs.

The aliens moved their bulbous heads extremely close to her pussy.

She glanced down at them, still twitching and sweating from the intense probing. "Um, is my pussy really that interesting?" She hoped they said "yes." Every girl wanted an interesting pussy.

One of the aliens dipped his finger inside her lips and then pulled it out, starting at the strange human juices coating it.

"Uh, that's called cum," she told him helpfully. "I just expelled a whole bunch of it."

He brought the finger to his lips, sampling her nectar.

Remy held her breath. Was he going to think she was yummy or icky?

He nodded to his companions. And all five of them stuck their fingers inside her at once.

"Oh fuck, that's so many fingers!" Fortunately, they didn't go too deep. Just far enough to get a sample of her pussy punch.

They all tasted it, agreeing with their colleague that she was tasty.

Remy beamed. Yes! Her pussy had passed the alien taste test. How many girls could claim that?

They continued to dip their fingers into her and suck off her juices. It was like she was a buffet and they could eat as much as they want.

"Help yourself, guys. I'm not going anywhere." She was still bound to the table and was at their mercy. But, so far, all they had done was give her the best climax of her life and make her feel really good about her pussy. These were cool aliens!

When they had their fill of her vagina, they unlocked her restraints and had her sit up.

"Oh, are we done already?" she asked. She kind of hoped they would continue exploring her body.

They flipped her over on her stomach and refastened her bonds. Okay, guess they weren't done. That was good. It was also good that they were strong. Surprisingly strong for how slight they were. That made Remy more eager to submit to them.

The same probe rose into place again.

"Oh, you want to fuck me in a different position? Good idea!" Remy was a big fan of trying out different sexual poses.

But then another probe joined its larger counterpart. And this one headed straight for her ass.

Oh fuck. Aliens really did love anal probing.

Yikes!

# Chapter 3

The small, silver probe approached Remy's ass.

"Wait! I've never done anal before."

The aliens didn't seem to be concerned.

Remy shrugged. Well, this was as good a time as any to try it. She had always been curious about shoving stuff up her butt.

Fortunately, the smaller probe rubbed against its big brother, getting lubricated in Remy's juices, which completely coated the big dildo. So at least it'd go in her ass a little easier.

She wondered why aliens loved butt fucking so much. She also wondered what other kinky things they were into. And how many of those kinky things they were going to make her do.

Since she was lying on her stomach, her ass created a nice mountainous peak compared to the rest of her body. Her former lovers couldn't seem to resist her booty, constantly wanting to spank and fondle it. Maybe that's why the aliens wanted to probe it. They might be as fascinated with her juicy butt as her human paramours.

The anal probe squeezed between her cheeks and reached her opening.

Remy tensed. Holy shit, she was about to lose her anal virginity to a bunch of aliens. This was either the strangest or greatest day of her life. Maybe both.

The alien sex toy pressed against her tiny opening. Remy gritted her teeth. She was too small. It wasn't going to fit.

It pierced her. "Holy fucking shit!!" Okay, it fit. But fuck was her ass super-tight around it.

She realized she was holding her breath and exhaled. It'd be easier to take if she just relaxed.

She tried, but it was hard when her ass was getting filled for the first time. The probe worked slowly into her, making her face contort as she groaned loudly.

The aliens studied her, obviously very interested in the faces she was making. But also interested in the way her ass contracted around the sex toy. They circled around the table, noting how her entire body was reacting to its first butt stuffing.

"I hope you guys are enjoying this. I don't do anal for just anyone, you know. Um, actually, I haven't done anal for anyone. So I guess you guys are special."

If they felt special, Remy couldn't tell. They merely nodded at each other as her ass wiggled around. Maybe she could reserve anal sex just for aliens. Not that she expected to meet a lot more of them. Unless these five told all their friends what an anal slut she was and she was passed around at alien parties as a fuck toy. That surprisingly excited her: a group of aliens having their way with her as everyone watched and saw what a sci-fi slut she was. Ahh, why was she thinking such kinky things? Okay, that wasn't that unusual for her, but these were especially kinky fantasies. Maybe getting fucked up the ass was unleashing her wild side.

The anal probe got all the way inside her.

"Uhhhhhhhhhhhhhh!" she moaned. "Oh my God, my ass feels so full! It's throbbing so bad!" It was true, her butt pulsated around the probe, trying to adjust to having a foreign object shoved up it.

That wasn't necessarily a bad thing. While it hurt somewhat at first, Remy was beginning to like the feeling of it in her ass. It felt kind of cozy, in an overwhelming "God, I'm such a slut!" way.

The larger probe pushed back into her pussy, joining its anal companion.

"Ohhhhhh, I'm so fucking stuffed!" She didn't know if the audio commentary was necessary: the aliens probably couldn't understand her. But she was always vocal when she got fucked. And her captors got animated every time she said something slutty, so she had a feeling they were enjoying it.

She whimpered on the table. Having her dual holes filled was overpowering. She couldn't think of anything except how much she wanted them to continue experimenting on her and make her squirt a bunch more.

"Ohhhh, I'm totally helpless," she told them. "You can fuck both my holes as hard as you want with your naughty probes and I can't do anything about it." Damn, she was getting hornier the more time she spent strapped to their exam table. She was learning new things about herself, like how much she enjoyed being submissive. Especially when she could be submissive to aliens!

Both probes went into action, pulling out of her pussy and ass and slamming back in simultaneously.

"Ohhhhhhh shit!!!" She hadn't been prepared for how intense the dual pounding would be. Who knew adding an anal component would generate so many more wonderful feelings inside her?

She moaned and groaned as the probes smashed her ass and pussy, increasing their speed and vibration with every thrust.

The aliens seemed to take particular interest in the way her ass cheeks rippled from the intense pounding. She managed to smile through her moans. Her ass was just as attractive to aliens as it was to humans. Yay!

The dildo ramming became so intense Remy thought she might black out. Her ass turned into sexy gelatin and her pussy a lake of submissive cum.

"Ohhh fuck, I love being probed by aliens!!" she squealed.

That confession made her captors turn up the devices so hard she gushed immediately. She flooded the table, her cum spilling onto the floor by the aliens' odd-shaped feet. They were kind of like human feet, but they lacked toes.

The pussy probe pulled out of her, letting her flow freely. Her juices shot in an arc behind her, soaking the rest of the exam table.

They left the anal probe inside her, probably thinking it would make her squirt more. They were right. Every time her ass contracted around the decadent alien device, she shot another blast of her juiciness.

"Oh God, you guys are going to make me become obsessed with getting my ass fucked!"

The aliens nodded as if that was the whole point. Sneaky aliens.

When she was done spilling, the pussy probe slipped back inside her. These aliens were not big on giving their test subject any breaks.

"Another round of pussy and ass fucking?" she asked hopefully.

They gathered in a tight circle, seeming to have some mental conversation.

The nearest one approached the head of the table, his crotch by Remy's mouth. The aliens had no genitalia, smooth gray skin covering where a sex organ would usually be.

That's what Remy thought anyway. She was shocked to see that skin open up and a gray penis emerge. It looked similar to a human cock, except it was way bigger than she expected for a creature of such small stature. And it kept growing before her eyes. Eyes that got very big when it finally reached its full girth. She couldn't believe he had such a huge cock. Was this common to his species?

She looked at his companions. All their cocks were out too. And they were all just as huge.

The alien penis throbbed in front of her.

So she had two big probes in her pussy and ass. She was tied up. And these aliens expected her to suck all five of their huge cocks.

Well, fuck.

# Chapter 4

The two phallic probes in Remy's pussy and ass pushed her forward, as if encouraging her to take the huge alien cock bobbing before her.

The alien waited expectantly, his colleagues looking on.

Remy stared at the head of the gray penis. It throbbed hypnotically, begging to be sucked.

Remy sighed. Oh what the heck, she had gone this far, letting them probe her pussy and take her anal virginity. Why not give this alien a blowjob? She'd be the only girl in her college who knew what alien dick tasted like. Unless her college attracted a lot of alien sluts.

She opened her mouth, and he moved the tip of his penis to her lips. Oh! He tasted different from a human. Less musky and more sweet. Remy could get behind a sweet-tasting dick!

She circled her tongue around his head, making him throb even harder. He moved closer, sticking more of his cock inside her mouth. She was glad he was going slow and didn't ram the whole thing in at once. Since she was tied up, she was really at his mercy. She liked that he was a gentleman alien. Assuming gentlemen liked tying girls up and shoving juicy probes in their tight holes.

She sucked on his dick, getting used to its consistency. It was smoother and more slippery than a human penis. But it was firmly planted it her mouth, so it wasn't going anywhere.

The pussy and ass probes began fucking her again, which made Remy greedy for more of his cock.

He gave her what she wanted, shoving the entire thing down her throat. She almost gagged before he pulled it out, her saliva dripping over his head and down her chin.

"Uhhhhh, more please!" The dildo devices pounding her ass and pussy made her crave his cock. It was only right she pleasure their alien appendages after all the pleasure their probes had given her.

She opened her mouth wide, indicating what she wanted.

He grabbed her long, brunette locks and thrust in and out of her mouth. Yes! This alien knew what he was doing. Remy loved it when people grabbed her hair while they fucked her.

The alien didn't moan or utter any sound, which was strange. Remy liked knowing her partners were enjoying her oral skills. A gasp, groan, calling her "his little slut." Anything. Of course, she had already surmised they communicated telepathically. So he could be telling his companions that this human female was a total whore and he loved fucking her. Man, that'd be so hot if that's what he was saying. Remy would totally be their alien whore. Wait, what? She would? Shit, those probes were really doing a number on her. Well, if she was going to be a whore, she might as well be an alien one. It was a lot more fun.

Her gray lover increased his speed, which told Remy he was indeed enjoying it. That and the fact that he gripped her hair more tightly. Not enough to hurt, but enough to tell her he wanted to ram her mouth until he emptied his balls of his alien cum. Actually, he didn't have balls. Maybe they were still inside his body like where his dick emerged from. Or maybe these aliens just didn't have any at all. Did that mean they could cum or not? Was it safe to swallow alien cum? And what would it taste like? Remy had so many questions as she got mouth fucked harder and harder. And got her pussy and ass pummeled fiercer and fiercer. The triple fucking was like nothing she had experienced. Alien sex was the best!

The alien's cock expanded, and he shot a thick, milky

liquid down her throat. Remy squealed, surprised at the sheer volume. But it actually tasted good. Almost like a sweetened coconut milk. No wonder these aliens were so good at turning human girls into their sluts: their cum was super-yummy!

She slurped him down while having her own climax from the dual pounding she was getting down below.

After she had swallowed an inordinate amount of his seed, he finally pulled out. She licked the remaining sweetness off her lips, gazing up at him.

"Wow, you're really good at cumming. Do you all cum like that?"

The second alien stepped up and filled her mouth. Guess she was going to find out.

He fucked her mouth just as hard as the first alien and came just as vigorously.

Remy panted after he was done. She had never felt so slutty before. These aliens were using her mouth as their personal plaything. But she didn't want them to stop. She wanted to take them all and prove that Earth girls could satisfy their alien horniness.

It also helped that the dual probes never stopped fucking her. So she was in a constant state of non-stop pleasure, punctuated with rapid bursts of climaxing.

The next three aliens fucked her mouth one after the other, not giving her a break in-between. They all spilled their seed down her throat, making her feel very full. She had never consumed this much cum in her life. Usually, she didn't even like swallowing. Except with girls. They usually tasted better than boys. But these aliens were too delicious to resist.

The probes pulled out of her, and she expelled one last glop of her juicy cum.

Her restraints popped free again and she got to her knees. "Are you guys getting the data you need from all your sexy experiments?" She assumed all this fucking was to learn about human sexuality and pleasure. Or maybe they just had a thing for Earth girls. Or maybe they had watched that 80s movie *Earth Girls Are Easy* and thought human females were all sluts. Not that Geena Davis was a slut in that film. But she was sexy!

A small seat slid out of the wall. The nearest alien grabbed her hips, lifted her off the table, and threw her face down over his lap as he sat on the seat.

And then proceeded to spank her. Hard.

"Owwww! What the heck? You guys are into kinky discipline?"

Another alien pointed to a holographic display that blipped into view before her. On it was a video of a hunky guy spanking a hot, naked girl. Oh shit. These aliens had been watching porn. That's what they chose to view to figure out humanity? Well, there were actually a lot worse things they could have watched.

Obviously, the aliens thought human girls loved being spanked. And, um, they weren't wrong. At least not about Remy. Getting her ass slapped really turned her on. She had a recurring fantasy of strong, sexy Amazons capturing her and spanking her submissive booty until she agreed to be their sex slave. But weird, gray aliens were just as good.

"Oh fuck, you're such a good spanker!" Remy had plenty of cushion to absorb the blows, but the alien was strong. Way stronger than a human. The spankings stung but also made her wet. Not that she wasn't wet enough from all her recent orgasms.

The other four aliens circled around and observed their colleague deliver the sexy punishment.

"Ouch! You guys really like to watch, huh?" She had never been spanked in front of an audience before. She hadn't realized it would turn her on this much. Who knew she was such an exhibitionist?

The alien voyeurs moved behind her, examining her reddening ass. They were very thorough in their research.

"Um, how many spankings am I going to get?" she asked out of curiosity.

The alien didn't reply but did increase the speed of his booty whacks.

"Ack! That many, huh?" She suffered them like she figured a good alien slut would, whimpering at each sexy blow.

The alien must have felt she had been punished enough, because he lifted her off his lap, facing her away from him.

Her legs straddled his, and between those gray legs rose his huge cock once more. A cock that was right below her pussy.

"Oh shit, are you going to... fuuuuuuuuuucccccckkkkkkkk!"

He rammed her down on his shaft, fully impaling her. She wasn't prepared to take his entire alien-ness at once. She bucked on his lap, her arms and legs flailing out of control from the sudden super-deep penetration. She could barely process how full her pussy was, how completely dominated she felt. In one huge thrust, this alien had captured her cunt and made it his. And she was going to let him do whatever he wanted to it.

What he wanted was to fuck it. Hard. He grabbed her waist and bounced her on his throbbing cock.

Her moans echoed off the smooth, metal walls of the ship. "Sooooo… fuuuccckkking… biiiigggggg!"

The holographic projection changed from the porn to a live shot of her being fucked by the alien.

Remy's eyes widened. What?! They were recording her? Oh no, was she going to be featured on some intergalactic whore website? Would she be the poster girl for how slutty human females were? Or was it just for their own personal use?

Remy had a hard time objecting due to what the alien was doing to her drenched pussy. He was fucking it silly, making her scream to the heavens, or at least to the alien gods.

She also found it very alluring watching herself get fucked. The holo-image showed her tits bouncing like crazy, the gray cock squishing inside her, her entire body a writhing mess of submissiveness. Damn, she looked pretty hot being fucked.

"C… can I… g… get a copy of th… this recording?" she asked between moans.

The aliens didn't respond. But they did zoom the holo into a closeup of her bouncing breasts and then a tight shot of her stuffed pussy.

"Y… you guys are r… really good at this alien porn stuff," she told them, the extreme closeups making her feel even sluttier.

The alien slammed her down one last time and shot his sticky seed up into her channel.

"Ohhhhhhh," she squealed. The feeling of his semen coursing into her vagina was even better than when it went down her throat.

She squirmed on his lap as he shot round after round into her. Then he raised her off his gray sword and let the others watch his cum drip out of her. Yup, they had learned way too much from porn. They were experts at turning women into naughty sluts.

He passed her to the next alien, who pushed her against the wall and fucked her from behind. The metal felt smoother than any Earth element. That was fascinating, but not as fascinating as how good the alien dick felt inside her.

She didn't know if they were still filming her, but she didn't care. She wanted to fuck these aliens for eternity. It was the most amazing sexual experience of her life. So what if she became an interstellar porn star? Maybe she'd get a cut of the royalties, and she wouldn't have to take out so many student loans.

The other three aliens fucked her in different positions. One made her ride him cowgirl style on the exam table. Another bent her over the table and slammed her pussy while spanking her. The last used Remy's flexibility to his advantage, laying her on her back with her legs spread wide and pressed to the floor on either side of her head. He slammed down on top of her, getting particularly deep, and filled her to overflowing.

Remy lay on the floor, exhausted and covered in alien cum. The intense fucking plus being up all night for the movie marathon sent her quickly into dreamland.

***

She woke on a metallic gray bed. A bed that had no mattress or cushions but was somehow still comfortable. Alien technology was cool!

She was in a small room that she guessed served as

personal quarters on the ship. She sat up and stretched. She felt pretty good considering she had just been fucked out of her mind by five aliens with huge cocks. She thought she'd be more sore. Maybe alien semen had rejuvenative effects. If so, she'd have to gulp down a bunch more of it.

She was still naked but her body was clean of the cum that had sluttily stained it. That was nice of the aliens to clean her. And let her sleep. She had no idea how long she was out. She hadn't seen any windows in the craft so didn't know if it was light out yet.

She was in mid-stretch, once again thrusting out her breasts, when the door slid open alien-spaceship-style, and two of her gray lovers walked in.

They took one look at her outstretched tits, and their cocks sprang from inside their bodies, growing to their full lengths.

The cocks twitched, beckoning her to come attend to them.

Remy pushed herself off the bed.

Looked like she had more sexy work to do.

# Chapter 5

The two aliens each put a hand on her ass, ushering her out of the room.

"Okay, okay, I'm coming." Well, she wasn't cumming at the moment, but she was sure she would be momentarily based on how eager these aliens were leading her down the gray corridor.

Even though it was cool inside the ship, their hands were pleasantly warm on her bottom.

"You guys are good ass grabbers," she told them.

They didn't reply but did squeeze her ass harder, making her utter a cute yelp.

A door slid open before them, presenting the bridge of the ship.

Remy marveled at the sight through the semi-circular windows: Earth. Her wondrously beautiful blue planet as seen from space.

She ran to the window, pressing her hands and breasts

against it. She had dreamed of being an astronaut when she was a kid, but never thought she'd actually get the chance to gaze down at the oceanic orb from orbit. Wait? She was in orbit? Holy shit! She had left Earth. That was crazy! Awesome but crazy. Why wasn't she floating around? And, more importantly, how would her boobs look bobbing in microgravity? The aliens must have artificial gravity technology. That was very advanced. Almost as advanced as their fucking techniques.

Speaking of, one of the aliens pressed his body against her, sliding his girthy alien cock all the way inside her pronounced pussy.

"Ohhhhhhh fuck!" she squealed, her breasts smashing harder into the glass and leaving large circular marks.

He seized her hips and fucked her hard. She moaned and whimpered as she gazed down at Earth.

"This is my favorite place to be fucked!" she confessed. A great view and a great fucking were a potent combination.

As usual, the other aliens gathered around to watch. That just got her wetter, and she was gushing in no time. Also gushing was the alien, shooting his thick liquid up into her cunt.

"Ohhhh God, there's so much alien cum inside me!" With what she had received before her nap and the current dose filling her, her pussy had welcomed more semen than it ever had in its life.

He passed her to the next alien, who turned her around and fucked her against the glass so she made ass marks on it. They were definitely going to need to clean their windshield after this. And their bridge with how much they were all leaking, including her.

She got a better view of the rest of the bridge as the alien slammed into her and fondled her breasts. It was spartan, with only two control consoles and no chairs. Though she surmised they may have more of the sneaky seats that emerged from the wall or floor.

"Th… thanks for showing me Earth," she moaned to the aliens. "It… it's beautiful."

Her current partner rewarded her by jizzing inside her and tossing her to another alien, who turned her sideways and raised her one leg straight up toward the ceiling. Thank goodness she was so flexible and could pull off sexy maneuvers like that.

He wrapped his arms around her raised leg and entered

her pussy. Bent perpendicular to her legs, Remy placed her hands on the glass and once again gazed out into space as her pussy received yet another deep alien probing.

The aliens continue to pass her around, fucking her in various positions like they had been studying the Kama Sutra. Oh crap, maybe they had studied that. She already knew they'd been watching porn to learn about human sexuality. So why not consult sensual texts too? Fuck, how many different positions were they going to try out on her? This was proving to be a very valuable sexual education: for both her and the aliens.

"Fuuuckkkk, I'm an alien sex toy!" she screamed as she was pulled off one huge cock and thrust onto another. A sex toy is exactly what she felt like, the aliens playing with her pussy like they owned it. She wanted them to own it. Wanted them to fuck and fill her until she was a moaning mess on the floor of their spaceship. She'd never be able to watch Star Trek the same way, constantly fantasizing about what Mr. Spock could do to her with his Vulcan strength. Okay, she may have already fantasized about that, as well as lots of other sexy aliens, especially the blue and green ones!

After many rounds of fucking, she sat on the floor, her

back against the windows overlooking Earth. Her legs were spread, letting the alien cum seep out of her.

One of the aliens lay on his back near her, his cock rising to full mast.

"Man, you guys have amazing stamina," Remy remarked.

The alien gazed at her expectantly.

"Let me guess, you want me to sit on your big dick again. You aliens are very horny."

He continued to stare.

"Okay, okay. My new rule is, I never say no to alien dicks." As rules go, it was a pretty good one. Alien dicks were hard to come by after all.

She crawled to him and straddled him cowgirl style, sinking onto his meaty member.

"Ahhhhhh," she sighed, loving the now familiar warmth of space cock.

Another alien pressed his cock against her ass.

"What?! You want to fuck me in both holes at once?"

The aliens' expression never changed, but she was learning how to read them. The one behind her seemed to indicate that of course they expected her to take their cocks in both holes. She was a huge alien slut after all.

Remy couldn't deny that, not after everything she let them do to her. But she was still worried.

"Okay, I know you used your sexy probe in my ass. But that was way smaller than your penis. You're huge!"

His penis bobbed up and down in response. Apparently, just like human males, aliens liked having their dicks complimented.

The alien spanked her. Then again, but harder.

"Ow! Okay, okay, you can fuck me in the ass. Just go slow, please."

Luckily, the alien's shaft was fully coated in her juices from all the pussy fucking he had given her, so it was well lubricated. Remy still didn't know how it was going to fit. She had just lost her anal virginity to their sexy probe a short while ago and now she was about to graduate to a full-on huge anal blasting. These aliens had turned her into the biggest whore in the galaxy. Well, she hadn't met any other intergalactic whores, so she had no comparison, but she felt pretty slutty.

He pressed it against her opening. Her ass resisted, screaming at her that the foreign object was way too big. Ah, what did it know?

"C'mon butt, take this juicy alien cock!" She didn't usually talk to her booty, but it obviously needed some encouragement.

It opened wider, allowing the alien penis to pierce its ultra-tightness.

"Holy shiiiiiiiittttttttt!" Remy wailed. "It's so fucking huge in my ass!"

The alien below throbbed in her pussy, evidently turned on by her slutty screams. The wonderful feeling in her loins helped her take more of the cock in her ass. It pushed in farther, opening her behind wider than she thought possible.

She clutched the alien beneath her, groaning and whimpering and praying she could take his friend's entire hugeness.

"Oh God, I'm an alien anal slut!" she cried when he got all the way inside her. Her entire body trembled, her insides completely dominated by the two alien cocks. She couldn't think of anything except how utterly submissive she felt, how her pussy and ass were meant to be stuffed by these thick, gray dicks.

Two other aliens moved to either side of her, their erections bobbing before her.

"Oh, you guys want to be fucked too, huh?" Remy couldn't refuse. It wasn't right for her to pleasure two of them and leave the rest out.

She took each of them in one hand, jerking off their smooth shafts.

The fifth alien knelt in front of her, pressing his cock against her lips.

She smiled. Of course, he wanted a blowjob. He wasn't going to let his alien mates have all the fun.

She opened her mouth and let him in. He tasted just as good as before, and she happily sucked him off. At the same time, she continued giving handjobs to the two aliens, while the other two plowed her pussy and ass like they were alien farmers.

Remy moaned into the huge cock in her mouth. She couldn't believe she was fucking five aliens at once. She had never been with more than one partner at a time before. These aliens had turned her into Orgy Girl! The sluttiest superhero in the galaxy!

Besides all the alien cocks in her, there were alien hands on her hips, ass, and hair. She was being felt up all over as she was being filled all over. Being an alien slut was the best!

The triple penetration provided more proof the aliens had some kind of mind meld: they thrust fully into her simultaneously with every stroke. Which made Remy feel more stuffed than she thought possible. It was difficult to focus on jerking off the two thick cocks in her hands, but she did her best. She was determined to make all five of her alien lovers cum at the same time. That had to set some kind of record, at least for Earth girls.

Those cocks between her fingers expanded and pulsated, as did the ones in her mouth, pussy, and ass. And using their amazing mind meld, all five aliens came at the same time.

Remy squirmed and squealed as three thick streams of semen flowed into her. It was her first experience receiving cum in her ass. It tickled and made her feel like her ass was meant to get daily cum deposits.

The two aliens she was jerking off came all over her tits. The other three wanted in on the fun, so they pulled out of her and shot their loads across her face, stomach, thighs, and ass.

She collapsed to the floor. The aliens stood over her and continued to coat her in their sticky seed. She took it like a good slut. She couldn't really move. She was exhausted from how many times they had fucked her, especially the five-way fucking they had just given her.

She twitched on the spaceship floor, leaking their cum out of her pussy and ass while more of it marked her body.

"Oh wow, I just pleasured five aliens at the same time." She obviously didn't have to tell them that, but a part of her felt like she needed to confess it.

Her confession seemed to spur a new round of climaxes from them. They drenched her writhing form, cumming way longer than any human could.

Remy glanced down her cum-covered body. "Holy shit, I'm so sticky. How do you guys keep that much cum inside you?"

They didn't answer but they did return the favor.

They knelt around her, ten hands roaming her breasts, thighs, and pussy. They were particularly attentive to her clit, which had escaped its hood and was throbbing in anticipation.

She felt like a piece of sexy meat, the aliens fondling her to their heart's content. Luckily, that fondling led to lots of squirting.

She let loose her cum as they fingered her pussy and clit. They were so skilled at pleasuring her, a huge pool formed between her legs in seconds.

Two of the aliens thrust their heads between her legs, lapping up her nectar. All five of them took turns licking her, seemingly never satiated with her tangy punch.

So she kept cumming for them and they kept drinking her human female sweetness.

She screamed and writhed on the floor, thinking how much she loved aliens. Their love of her pussy juice made her feel great about herself. If any future lovers didn't want to go down on her, she'd tell them, "Hey, if it's good enough for aliens, it should be good enough for you."

When they were done, the aliens fell asleep on her. Two on her breasts, two on her thighs, and one right between her legs with his head on her pussy.

"Oh, guess I'm your sexy pillow. Sure, why not." She closed her eyes, feeling rather cozy with five aliens snuggled around her.

She dozed off almost instantly, her energy drained from all her climaxing.

***

She woke to the movement of bodies beside her. The aliens helped her to her feet, then pointed out the window at Earth.

"You're taking me back home?" she guessed. "Okay. I'm really going to miss you guys. And your amazing cocks!"

She hugged the nearest alien. He didn't know what to do, likely unfamiliar with human shows of warmth. The problem with using porn as a lesson in humanity is that it was all about fucking. Not that Remy thought that was a problem. She loved all the fucking the aliens had given her.

She moved his hands around her, showing him how to hug. Then lowered his hands to her ass, where he gave her a delicious squeeze. That kind of hug the alien fully understood.

She hugged the rest in turn, each one squeezing her juicy butt. It was a great way to say goodbye.

They ushered her into a cylindrical device set into an alcove of the bridge. It was big enough for one person, or alien, and had circular pads on the top and bottom.

"Is this some kind of pod that will take me back to Earth?" she asked.

One of the aliens activated the device. The circular pads glowed blue-white, emanating a pleasant warmth.

Remy waved to them. "Um, okay, bye. If you're ever near

Earth again, feel free to abduct me for more fucking."

The aliens awkwardly raised their hands, which only had four fingers, and tried to replicate her gesture. They also raised their cocks, their erections a sexy send off to their human slut.

The blue-white light engulfed Remy and, in the blink of an eye, she was back on Earth, standing in the same spot in Old Man Smithers's field.

Holy crap! The aliens had transporter technology like on Star Trek. They were so freakin' advanced! She had so many questions she wanted to ask them. She probably should have asked while she was on their ship, but she was too busy fucking them. And they couldn't understand her anyway. Sex was really the greatest universal language.

She looked heavenward, seeing if she could spot their ship rocketing off into space. But all she saw were the twinkling stars. They were probably still cloaked to ensure no humans detected them. Except for the human they had chosen to fuck super-hard.

The wind blew Remy's hair across her face and made her nipples harden. And that's when she realized she was still naked. Those aliens had stolen her clothes! Well, she supposed it was a fair trade with all the amazing sex they had given her.

She was also still covered in their cum. Yikes! She had to clean off. She definitely couldn't explain this to her parents.

A bright light illuminated the field. At first she thought the aliens might have returned. *Yes! More fucking!* But then she realized it was a light attached to a nearby barn.

"Who in hell is out in my field at this time of night?" Old Man Smithers bellowed.

Ack! Remy covered her chest. She couldn't let him catch her naked and coated in alien cum.

She sprinted through the field, away from the light and Smithers's curses.

She got far enough where she'd knew she'd be safe. She sat against a tree, gazing at the stars.

Wondering when she'd get to fuck aliens again.

# Chapter 6

Remy slept for a long time. Being fucked by five horny aliens really wore her out.

But she felt surprisingly good when she woke in the afternoon. It was almost as if alien cum was like an energy drink for her pussy.

She threw the sheets off and stretched her nude body. She usually didn't sleep in the buff but after showering last night she immediately plopped onto her bed and fell asleep. The sheets had felt nice against her bare body. So maybe she'd sleep without clothes from now on. Oh no, was alien cum making her a slut and a nudist? A slutty nudist? Well, there were a lot worse things to be.

She showered again, needing to vigorously scrub her pussy after all the alien fucking. Of course, that led to her fantasizing about the aliens taking her in the shower, all five of them ravishing her as the warm water cascaded over her submissive body.

She came hard, fingers buried deep inside. Her climax made her shake so much, she slid to the floor, legs flailing, pussy squirting. It was wonderful.

After drying off, she threw on shorts and a Cowboy Bebop T-shirt and checked her phone. Lily had texted her, asking what the aliens were like. It took Remy a minute to remember they had joked about that before she parted ways with her two friends last night. If only Lily knew how prophetic their kidding had been. Should Remy tell her best friend she got dominated by five aliens with huge cocks? Would she believe her? She'd probably think Remy was just having one of her kinky sci-fi fantasies she was always sharing. But this fantasy had totally come true.

She was considering what to text Lily when she spotted the reminder she had put in her phone. She had been looking for a way to earn money over the summer to help pay for her junior year of college. She had spotted an online ad looking for people her age to be part of a psychology experiment. She didn't know what the experiment was, but the compensation was pretty good, so she figured it was worth checking out. She had almost forgotten she was supposed to swing by today.

She hurried out of the house, grabbing some chocolate chip cookies her mother had left out. Her mom made the most delicious cookies. Both her parents were at work, so she had the house to herself. Helpful for when she masturbated in her room. She didn't have to worry about how loudly she moaned and screamed.

Remy made the short drive to the address on the ad, which was a mostly abandoned strip mall. Well, that wasn't sketchy at all.

A chime rang when she walked in to the makeshift reception area. Great. More sketchy vibes.

"Um, hello?" she called out tentatively.

She received no response.

She was about to leave when a woman poked her head out from another door. "Oh, hi there!" She was about ten years older than Remy, wore glasses, and had a cute geekiness to her. Totally Remy's type of girl. The woman smiled warmly, pushing her glasses up with her finger. "You must be Remy."

Remy shook the proffered hand. "That's me! Nice to meet you."

"You too! I'm Dr. Samantha Shen. Thanks so much for coming!" The Doc's infectious smile put Remy at ease. It didn't hurt that she found the woman very attractive. She was Asian, probably Chinese from her last name, and had short black hair that perfectly framed her cute face. It was hard to tell under her lab coat, but Remy was sure the Doc had a great body.

"My pleasure, Dr. Shen."

"Oh, you can call me Sam."

Remy almost replied that the Doc could call her "alien slut" but she kept that to herself.

"Great shirt!" Sam commented. "I love Cowboy Bebop."

Remy beamed. This was a woman after her own heart. Whatever experiment she wanted to do, Remy was onboard. "Yes! It's amazing. And Faye's so cool!"

"And sexy!" Sam replied with an impish grin. Oh crap, was she flirting with Remy? Did she want to do a sexy cosplay where Remy dressed as Faye Valentine and let Sam handcuff her and experiment on her pussy? Because Remy would be totally down with that. She would? Yikes, the alien fucking must be making her hornier than usual. Not that she normally wasn't pretty horny. But she usually didn't fantasize about being super-submissive right after meeting someone.

"So, what are you studying?" Remy asked, curious about

the experiment.

"Sex!"

"What?!"

"Sex. And orgasms."

Remy's eyes widened. Holy crap! "You're a sex doctor?"

"Yup. Well, a sexual psychologist."

"You have an amazing job!"

Sam giggled. "Thank you! You have an amazing body."

Remy blushed, unprepared for Sam's frank admission. "Oh, um, thanks."

"An amazing body to experiment on!"

"Wait? You want to do sex experiments on me?"

"Oh yeah. I can tell you're a huge squirter."

Now Remy really blushed. How did she know that? Last night was her first time squirting. Though she did it a lot thanks to the aliens' sexual prowess. So much that her pussy was like a fire hose spewing cum. "H... how do you know that?"

"Oh, I can always tell when I meet a fellow nymphomaniac."

"I'm not a nymphomaniac!" Remy protested.

"Are you sure? You have the look of a woman who just

experienced a huge sexual awakening."

Remy gasped. Did Sam have Professor X mind powers? How did she know Remy just had the most amazing and hardcore sex of her life? Was Remy emitting some kind of joyous glow because of the wonderful alien orgy? "Well, I, um, did just have my first orgy last night."

"Yes! Good for you. Aren't they awesome?"

"Soooo awesome."

"What else did you do?"

"Ack! How are you so good at knowing all this stuff?"

"It's my job, remember?"

"Oh, right. Well, I… sort of just lost my anal virginity."

"Sort of?"

"Okay, I lost my anal virginity big time. Their cocks were so huge!"

"Ooh, multiple cocks in your ass? You little slut!"

"No! Well, yeah, but not at the same time."

"I'm so jealous. There's nothing quite like a good butt fucking!"

Remy smiled. She was glad this woman shared her kinky delight in getting her butt stuffed. It was nice to be able to confess all the decadent things she had done. She had to leave out the alien part of course. But that didn't mean she couldn't describe every dirty thing they did to her.

"C'mon, let me show you the testing area." Sam grabbed Remy's wrist and yanked her through the door.

Remy was shocked at the contents of the spacious room: it was filled with all manner of sex machines containing harnesses, restraints, and dildos galore.

"Oh my goodness!" she exclaimed, her eyes so big she felt like she couldn't blink.

Sam nudged her. "Pretty great, right? I built all these machines myself."

"You did?"

"Yup. I'm a little obsessed with sex."

"I can see that." Remy couldn't take her gaze off all the decadent devices, fantasizing about what they could do to her. "So, you want me to try out one of them for your experiment?"

"Nope. I want you to try out all of them!"

"All of them? But there are so many!"

"Didn't you say you just had a big orgy last night?"

"Um, yeah, but…"

"This is just like that, but with machines instead of

people."

Remy continued to scan the sensual contraptions. Sam made a good point. And the aliens had probed both her holes with their own sex machine last night. That had made her super-horny for the rest of her fucking sessions with them. It would be good research to compare human-made fuck machines to alien ones. And she'd be getting paid to have sex. Wait, did that make her a prostitute? Not if it was for science, right? If she was going to be a courtesan, she'd prefer being an alien one.

"Okay, I'll do it!" she announced.

Sam thrust her hand over her head. "Yes! I knew you were my kind of slut the moment I saw you."

Remy blushed again. What the heck, one night with aliens and everyone knew how much of a whore she was? Geez.

"Take off your clothes," Sam commanded.

"Right in front of you?"

"I'm going to be seeing you naked the entire time you're on the machines so no need for modesty. Plus, I love seeing girls strip!"

Remy smiled. This was one sexy and horny scientist. But she couldn't fault her logic: Remy loved watching girls strip too.

There were no windows in the room so she didn't have to worry about any sneaky peepers peeping on her. She'd be putting on a show for a one-woman audience.

Remy took off her sneakers and socks and fidgeted. For some reason, she was more nervous to strip in front of one human scientist than five aliens. Of course, the aliens had already removed her clothing when she came to on their ship. So she didn't have to perform for them. At least not in that way. She certainly performed for them sexually in every way imaginable.

"Don't be shy," Sam encouraged. "You're crazy hot!"

Remy's cheeks reddened once again. "Oh, thanks, you're really sweet." She had a weakness for girls who complimented her body. So she was definitely going to strip for this sexy scientist.

She pulled her T-shirt over her head, letting her perfectly tanned breasts bounce free.

"Ooh," Sam marveled. "Now those are some nice tits. And no bra. You are a kinky slut!"

"I like to let my girls fly free," Remy agreed.

"You should. Your girls are fantastic! Now turn around

and show me your ass."

Remy did as she was told, wondering why she was obeying Sam's every command. The scientist was enjoyably chipper but also had the ability to make Remy do whatever she wanted. Maybe that was part of her sexy psychology training. What a sneaky scientist sexpot!

She inched her hips back and forth as she slid her tight shorts past her hips and pushed them down her legs, revealing her juicy butt clad in a tiny black thong. She had unconsciously chosen it when she got dressed, perhaps influenced by how slutty the aliens had made her feel.

"Wow, what an ass! No wonder everyone wants to fuck it."

Remy glanced over her shoulder. Sam was salivating at her booty's juiciness.

"Oh, I'm sure not everyone wants to fuck it."

"Trust me, they do. And my machines are going to fuck it really hard."

"The sex machines are for anal too?"

"Of course. Aren't you craving more ass fucking after your first time?"

"Oh fuck, yeah!" Remy covered her mouth, surprised by

how forcefully she answered. "I mean, um, that'd be nice."

Sam giggled. "You're adorable. Now take those panties off please."

Remy slipped them down her smooth, toned legs and stood naked before the scientist.

She fidgeted, not knowing where to put her hands. Part of her wanted to cover up, part wanted to show off her assets to the naughty doctor.

Sam took in her entire nudeness. "You are gorgeous."

Remy smiled. This Doc was one heck of a flatterer. "Are you just saying all this so I'll let you fuck me on all your sexy machines?"

"Yup. Is it working?"

"Oh yeah."

"Great! But I also mean it. You're one of the most beautiful women I've ever seen."

Remy felt a wonderful warmness between her legs. If Sam kept saying stuff like that, she was going to beg the scientist to fuck her on and off the machines. "Okay, Doc, my body belongs to you. Where do you want me?"

Sam snatched her wrist again and yanked her over to the first sinful contraption.

Remy gazed at it. She was about to be bound and fucked by a sex machine for the second day in a row. Well, technically the same day as it was after midnight when the aliens had abducted her.

Either way, she was going to be helpless, subjected to robotic pussy pounding.

Fuck, yeah!

# Chapter 7

"Ta-da! The Booty Blaster 3000!" Sam waved her arm in front of a strange contraption: it was shaped like a water wheel but much smaller, with flexible plastic paddles as its spokes.

"Wow," Remy replied, not knowing what else to say. She didn't have experience with sex machines outside of the kinky ones the aliens had used on her.

"Cool, right? It can deliver up to three thousands spankings per minute."

"Three thousand?! That's so many!"

"Not for an ultra butt slut."

"I'm not an ultra butt slut!"

"Are you sure? With that curvy booty, you were born to be one."

Remy wiggled her nose, wondering if that's what her parents thought the day she came into the world. Probably not. Parents usually didn't dream of how slutty their daughter would become. But, c'mon, if it was for important experiments like Sam was doing or to ensure galactic peace with aliens, wasn't her sluttiness justified? Well, Remy could tell herself that. "Um, thanks, I think. But I can't take that many spankings at once."

"Don't worry, we'll work up to it. And this machine will have fun with your pussy too."

"Great! My pussy likes having fun."

"I bet. It's super-cute."

Remy squeezed her legs together, her pink pussy blushing from the compliment. "So… what do I do?"

"Kneel here and spread your thighs."

Remy did as instructed, kneeling between sets of silver metal rings.

Sam slipped black rope through the rings and around Remy's ankles, calves, and thighs. The rope was soft and pleasantly tickled Remy's skin.

"Th… that feels kinda nice."

"I knew you'd like being tied up," Sam replied. "I see you're already getting wet."

Remy glanced between her legs. Oh shit, her pussy was indeed glistening. She was more excited than she thought to let Sam experiment on her. "S… sorry."

"Don't apologize. It's fascinating for my research. Now I know bondage turns you on. The more info I have to make you a slut the better."

"What?! Dr. Shen, I thought you wanted to see how these machines affected people's orgasms."

"I do. But if they make you have lots of orgasms, that will make you feel really slutty. So the sluttier you become, the better my machines are working. Make sense?"

"Um, I guess." Remy thought this doctor was a little kooky, but she was pretty and friendly. And Remy never said no to free orgasms.

"The ropes are attached to pulleys, so I can fully control your body."

Remy shivered. She liked the idea of this sexy doc controlling her body. "O… okay."

Sam tied Remy's wrists together, then attached the loose rope to a metal ring dangling from the ceiling. More rope led from the ring to a track along the ceiling where a metal slider could move back and forth.

The kinky scientist pulled the other end of the rope and yanked Remy's arms above her. She raised Remy until her arms were fully extended and she could feel the fabric around her thighs tighten. She was completely helpless, unable to move up or down.

Sam stepped back to appreciate her handiwork. "How do you feel?"

"I... like I'm totally at your mercy."

"Great! That's how I like my sluts, er, I mean, my test subjects."

Remy bit her lip, more convinced that Dr. Shen really just liked slutting up co-eds. But Remy's nipples were hard, her pussy was wet, and she really wanted to be fucked. So she was completely fine with the kinky doc experimenting on her.

"Oh wait," Sam continued. "Let's emphasize that juicy ass of yours." She yanked the rope connected to Remy's wrists, pulling her upper body forward. This made her ass stick out at the Booty Blaster.

Sam walked behind Remy to examine her naked booty. "There. Much better. Perfect spanking position."

Remy tingled, feeling even more helpless. "Y... you won't go too hard, will you?"

"Not at first. We'll work out way up to it. But don't worry, I bet you'll be begging for the top speed in no time."

Remy thought she might be right. She had begged the aliens to fuck her with their huge alien cocks again and again.

Dr. Shen circled Remy, studying her closely.

"Um, is everything okay?" Remy asked. "Aren't we going to begin the experiment?"

"Yup. I just wanted to take in every morsel of your gorgeous, nude body."

Remy's cheek reddened. "Hey, is this a real experiment or am I just putting on a peep show for you?"

"Sorry! It's a real experiment, I promise. I've just never had such a beautiful test subject."

Remy's face got even rosier. "Oh, um, th… that's really sweet of you to say." Even though the doc was a little weird, Remy had to admit she loved the flattery.

"So does that mean you'll put on a peep show for me after the experiments?"

"What?! No! I mean, um, maybe. If you fuck me really good, I'll probably agree to almost anything."

"Yes! Then I'll give you the best fucking of your life!"

Remy sighed. Why had she confessed that? She had just given Sam free reign over her body. Well, the way she was bound, Sam already had free reign over her. And what was wrong with putting on a sexy show for the hot doc? She put on a really kinky one for five horny aliens.

Sam moved the Booty Blaster into position, then hopped on a stool and opened her laptop. "Here we go!" She tapped a key.

The spanking wheel whirled into motion, each rectangular paddle gently whacking Remy's ass. They were like love taps, softly jiggling Remy's sexy cheeks.

Sam looked up from her computer. "How does that feel?"

"P… pretty nice. I like how there's so many paddles that I'm constantly getting spanked." The plastic spanking instruments were evenly spaced apart on the wheel, striking her booty one after the other.

"You'll really like it when I speed it up." Sam hit another key, and the machine went twice as fast.

Remy grunted and groaned, the slaps coming harder and faster. It felt like she was getting firm spankings from a dominant lover who wanted to show her how to be submissive.

"Looks like you're enjoying that," Sam said gleefully. "Let's go even faster!"

"Ohhhh fuck!" Remy cried as the machine sped up. It was

spanking her much faster than a human could. Her cheeks were jiggling and bouncing and turning very red. "I've never been spanked like this before!"

"And you can't stop it, can you?"

"No!"

"Why not?"

"Because I'm tied up and totally helpless!" Remy's pussy spasmed at her slutty confession. It obviously loved being helpless and didn't want her ass to have all the fun.

"So being tied up is helping you feel slutty?"

"Oh God, yes!"

"Great! And how about the Booty Blaster?"

"Ow, fuck! It… it's making me feel like my ass belongs to you."

"Oh my goodness, that's fantastic!" Sam clasped her hands together and had a sexy, maniacal gleam in her eyes. Remy wondered if she had stumbled upon a mad scientist. Though most mad scientists weren't obsessed with giving girls orgasms. This was the kind of scientist Remy could get behind.

Speaking of behinds, Remy's was getting smacked insanely hard. But she didn't want it to stop. It was making her so fucking horny and making her pussy so fucking wet.

Sam noticed. "Looks like your cute vagina is ready for some action." She pressed more keys and a panel in the floor slid open. A white vibrating wand emerged and rose until it pressed against Remy's pussy and clit.

Remy gasped when it touched her. She had a similar one at home, and it was great at giving her awesome orgasms.

Except this one was way more powerful. As soon as Sam turned it on, it vibrated Remy's pussy and clit so powerfully, she immediately climaxed. And not just any climax: she squirted clear across the room.

"Ohhhhhhh fuuuuuuuckkkkkkkk!" Guess aliens weren't the only ones who could make her squirt. Or maybe they unlocked something in her, so now she could expel her juices every time she came. Oh shit, she was going to make such a mess everywhere she went. Well, not everywhere. It wasn't like she was cumming twenty-four hours a day. Though if Sam had her way, she very well might.

"Holy shit!" the cute scientist exclaimed. "You're a squirter! That's awesome!"

"Th... thanks," Remy replied, still squirting. "I just discovered I could do it."

"Best discovery ever! Since you're squirting, you don't mind if I turn both machines up to their highest setting, right?"

"Ohhhhhhhh God, turn them up as high as you can! Fuck and spank me like I'm your personal whore!" Remy wasn't sure why she was a personal whore instead of a regular whore. But she supposed the alternative would be a public whore, where she would get passed around to everyone in the town square. If the town square consisted of the sexy aliens from last night, Remy would totally be a public whore. And she kind of was already, letting all five of the creatures fuck her at the same time.

"Woohoo!" Sam replied in that gleeful, maniacal way of hers. "My inventions are working better than I expected. Personal whore mode coming up!"

Remy thought she was at maximum bliss before, but that was nothing compared to when the devices were turned to their highest settings. The Booty Blaster became a blur of motion, its paddles moving so fast Remy was easily receiving three thousands spankings per minute. And the vibrator wand caused such a seismic earthquake in her pussy, it registered as a 9.9 on the Sexual Richter Scale.

She screamed, squirted, screamed some more. And told Dr. Shen whatever she wanted to hear.

"Are you a butt slut?" the kinky doc asked.

"I'm a butt slut!"

"Are you a pussy slut?"

"I'm a huge pussy slut!"

"Are you the biggest slutty co-ed on Earth?"

"Fuck, yes!! No one's a bigger slut than me! Please keep making me cum!" Remy couldn't believe she was blurting out such whorish things. But she was in such a state of sexual delirium, she would have said anything Sam wanted. At least she didn't admit she was the biggest slut in the galaxy like she did to the aliens.

"Okay, you are definitely my favorite test subject of all time."

Remy smiled through her sex faces. She liked being people's favorite, even if it was someone's favorite slut.

"Let's give you one last huge orgasm and see if you can hit the far wall with your juices." Sam pulled the ropes, so Remy's torso was yanked backward and her pussy aimed at the target.

She returned to her laptop and tapped a key with a

flourish.

And Remy had an orgasm like no other. She tried to scream, but no words came out. Her climax had rendered her speechless.

Her pussy, however, was not speechless. It sent a large, single stream of cum arcing across the room until it splattered against the wall and windows.

Remy hung loosely from the ropes, totally spent, continuing to squirt out small blasts of cum.

Sam turned the machines off and came over, marveling at Remy's leakage. "Wow, you're still squirting."

Remy trembled uncontrollably. "I… I can't stop. Y… your machines are amazing."

"I knew you'd like them. And your slutty confessions were wonderful. They gave me so much data on what people are willing to say when being fucked out of their minds."

"Oh God, I'm so embarrassed I said all that."

"Don't be. It was hot as hell!"

"R… really? Oh fuck, I'm squirting again!"

Sam watched Remy add to the growing pool underneath her. "Really."

"O… okay, I'm glad I'm helping with your research."

"Wanna help some more?" Sam had that familiar glint in her eyes.

"If it means I'll get fucked like that, heck yeah!"

"You're my kind of girl!"

"So what machine are you going to strap me to next?" Remy surveyed the many decadent contraptions in the room.

"Actually, I want to skip right to my most recent invention. Now that I know how much you love to be submissive."

Remy nodded. She was discovering lately just how submissive she could be.

Sam pressed another key on her computer and the wall behind Remy slid open. Mechanical stomping sounds approached her.

She craned her neck and was finally able to see Sam's invention.

It was a large mechanized creature with metal arms and legs and a steel head. But most importantly, it had a huge prosthetic dick.

Holy shit. It was a sex robot.

And it was staring right at Remy.

# Chapter 8

"Meet the T-69!" Sam proclaimed, gesturing at the metal monstrosity towering over Remy.

"Like The Terminator?" The original was one of Remy's favorite films, and she could easily quote a bunch of lines from it. This robot was larger and bulkier than the classic Terminator exoskeleton and didn't look so exoskeletony. Its metal joints and limbs were covered with smooth, hardened plastic. Its head looked more like Baymax from Big Hero 6 than the scary Terminator skulls.

"Yup. But more like a Sexinator. Sent back in time to dominate your pussy! Except for the sent back in time part since I just created it in the present." Sam was obviously very proud of her invention.

"Wow." Remy marveled at the robot, especially the ridiculously huge prosthetic cock between its legs. "Have you tried it out yet?"

"Nope. That's what you're here for."

"Wait? I'm going to be the first test subject."

"Yeah, that's what you signed on for, remember."

Remy tapped her lips. She supposed that was true. "Um, I guess, but how come I have to be the very first?"

"Because you're the hottest test subject I've ever had," the sexy doc replied, ogling Remy's nude body.

Remy smiled. That was a very good explanation.

"Plus everyone else ran away when they saw my kooky sex inventions."

Remy rolled her eyes. She liked the first explanation better.

Sam's phone alarm blared with the theme to Knight Rider. Remy appreciated the sexy doc's choice in TV shows.

"Oh crap, I almost forgot about this funding meeting. Gotta go!"

"Wait!" Remy called after her. "What am I supposed to do?"

"Let my robot fuck the shit out of you. T-69, turn her into a slut!"

"Affirmative," the robot replied in its robot voice. "Slut mode activated." Remy didn't realize it could talk.

"What?!" she replied in shock to Sam. But it was too late. The doc was already out the door.

The robot loomed over her.

"Um, hello, I'm Remy."

"Affirmative. You are Remy the Slut."

"What? No, I'm just Remy." Stupid Sam calling her a slut. Now the robot thought that was part of her name.

"You are just Remy the Slut. Understood."

She sighed. Oh, whatever. "Okay, fine, I'm Remy the Slut. What, um, are we supposed to do?"

"My mission is to fuck you until you beg to become my sex toy."

Remy gasped. "What kind of mission is that?!"

"One my creator believes is vital to humanity."

Remy wrinkled her nose. Of course, the kinky doc would think creating sluts was the key to mankind's future.

"Are you prepared to become a sex toy?" it asked.

"Um, I guess." Remy had certainly become the sex toy of the aliens, and that proved to be a lot of fun. She let them pass her around like her pussy, mouth, and ass existed only to please their alien cocks. Was it really any weirder to let a robot dominate her? Especially one with such a big dick.

"I need a clear affirmative or negative," the robot stated.

"Oh, sorry. Sure, I'm ready for you to fuck me and make

me your sex toy."

"Good. I detect your nipples are at 68% of their full length and your pussy is at 57% saturation. You are ready to be fucked, but we must get those levels to 100%."

Remy blushed furiously and covered her tits and crotch. She had never had a sex partner describe her naughty areas in such numerical terms. She also hadn't realized how turned on she had gotten during her weird chat with the robot. "You can detect all that?"

"Of course. I am programmed to fully analyze the human body to provide full orgasmic pleasure."

Full orgasmic pleasure? Remy liked the sound of that.

She put her hands down. "Okay, you can scan my nude body as much as you want."

The robot looked her up and down. Remy had a feeling her pussy saturation level just increased. Being ogled by a machine was exciting!

"According to my scans, your body is highly desirable to those attracted to the female form. The vast majority of humans you encounter should want to fuck you."

Remy's face had just returned to its normal color when her cheeks flushed again. Did that many people really want to have sex with her? Why wasn't she getting laid more often? "Oh, wow, that's, um, cool. Do you really think so?"

"Of course. My data is infallible. And you are the ideal age for fucking and breeding."

"You're going to breed me?!"

"No. Robots cannot breed. But many males will wish to do so with you."

Even more blushing. Remy definitely wasn't ready to have a baby. But she supposed it was nice that the robot thought so many guys wanted to knock her up.

"Fucking commencing." The robot grabbed Remy's waist with its thick, metallic fingers, hoisted her into the air, and thrust her down on its robot dick.

"Ohhhh fuck, you're so big!" Remy wailed. She should have known robots weren't into foreplay. It went right for the penetration.

"I am outfitted with instruments to make women become complete sluts."

"Uhhhhhhh," Remy moaned as it lowered her on its shaft. "It's working!"

"To become a proper slut, you must take all of my cock."

"All of it?! I don't know if I can." The robot was even

bigger than the aliens. And they had really put Remy's pussy to the test.

"Your pussy has the capacity to take it. Though it will fill your entire vaginal channel."

"Ohhhhhh, are you saying I have a tight pussy?"

"I believe that is the correct human vernacular."

"Th… thanks. You're a nice robot."

"I am merely stating facts. Now prepare to be fully penetrated."

Remy prepared. Not that you could really prepare for something that huge filling every inch of your pussy and making you feel like it was going to burst through your cervix.

"Oh God, T-69, I feel like you're going to explode out of me!"

"That is good. It should be making you feel like a slut."

"I definitely feel like a slut!"

"Then I will commence fucking your slutty pussy."

Remy's slutty pussy squeezed his dick. She loved it when robots talked dirty to her.

Its plastic-coated chest was too slippery to hang on to, but Sam had cleverly placed two rubber grips on its torso. Remy grabbed them and hung on for dear life.

It was good she did for the robot smashed her on its cock with a strength surpassing even the aliens'.

"Holy fuck, you're destroying my pussy!"

"Is my analysis correct that in this circumstance 'destroying' is a good thing?"

"So good! Great! Awesome! Fantastic!"

"Then I will destroy it further."

"Yes, please!" Remy was beginning to love this robot. It was polite and geeky, just how she liked her romantic partners. And its fucking ability was off the charts. Remy's ass was a jiggling mess as T-69 rammed her on its cock again and again. With every thrust, she thought it would break her pussy. But somehow she survived. And not only survived but begged for more.

"Please fuck me harder, T-69!"

"You must say the correct passphrase."

"Um, robots are cool?"

"That is an accurate statement but not the correct passphrase."

"Robots have big dicks?"

"That is closer but still not correct."

Remy groaned in frustration. She wanted it to fuck her harder. So hard that she'd black out. "Fuck me like the huge robot slut I am!"

"That is the correct passphrase."

Remy should have known it'd be something like that. But she didn't have time to think about it. She was getting jackhammered faster and harder than any human or alien had ever fucked her.

"Oh fuck, I'm cumming, I'm cumming, I'm cuuuuummmmmmmming!!!" She squirted all over the robot's dick. Hopefully, it was water resistant: the dick and the robot.

It lifted her off its huge appendage and held her flailing body aloft while she leaked all over the floor.

"Good. Expulsion of your sex fluids will lead to greater slutty behavior."

"Ohhhh fuck, it sure will!" Remy agreed, still flailing and still squirting. This robot was definitely going to make her its robot whore.

"Commencing next fucking position." Before Remy was done squirting, T-69 tossed her on a table and folded her legs up by her ears, pinning her arms beneath her.

"Are you able to move?" it asked her.

"N… no. I'm helpless."

"Good." It penetrated her again, and once again fucked the shit out of her. Remy could do nothing except take it. The robot was so strong she couldn't move at all. And fuck, did that make her hot. She wanted this amazing sex robot to force her into all sorts of kinky positions, making her beg for its cock until she became its sex slave.

"Oh God, so d… deep!" In her current position, it felt like her metal lover was even farther inside her, dominating her even more than it was during their first fucking.

"Do you enjoy deep fuckings?" it queried.

"Yes! I love it! Give me your whole cock!" Remy was losing all self-control. All she could think about was the wonderful robotic penis plumbing her wet human depths.

It plumbed her until she was leaking again. And she wasn't the only one leaking this time. T-69 ejaculated inside her.

Remy squealed in shock. Holy shit, this robot could cum? What the heck was robot cum like? It sure felt like real semen, except that her fuck buddy was unloading way more than a human could. "Oh my God, you're cumming inside me!"

"Yes. Please take it like a good slut."

Remy took it like a good slut. It felt too good not too. It helped that she was still having her own orgasms.

The robot filled her to overflowing. Then pulled out, but kept her pinned in her submissive position.

"Oh fuck, there's so much cum in me!" The way T-69 had her legs folded, the cum was stuck inside her rather than leaking out like normal.

"That is how it should be," it replied. "It will make you feel like a slut to hold my cum inside you."

Remy couldn't disagree with that assessment. "But how are you able to cum at all?"

"I am filled with 3.2 gallons of a water-based lubricant that resembles male semen."

"Oh, cool. Wait, you're going to shoot over three gallons of cum into me?"

"No. I am going to shoot cum both inside you and all over your exterior." To prove its point, it shot its creamy goodness across her tits.

"Oh, um, thanks." Remy didn't mind being covered in cum. But three gallons was a lot.

"You are welcome. And I will likely have to refill my reservoirs as my current cum capacity will not be enough."

"It won't?"

"Not to make you a true slut."

Remy gulped. What had she gotten herself into? But she did like the idea of being a true slut, especially to a dominant robot. "Is it okay if I let your cum leak out of me now?"

"Do you feel sufficiently submissive?"

"Yup."

"That is not the correct answer."

"Um, yes I feel sufficiently like a submissive slut and I can't wait to take more of your juicy robot cum."

"That is correct." It lifted her off the table and spread her legs, allowing her to empty her vagina of most of its sticky seed.

Remy squirmed and squealed. She had never had this much semen leak out of her before. This robot was making her feel like a total sex toy.

"I must record our next fucking session," T-69 informed her.

"What?! Y... you're going to video us having sex?"

"Correct. I must provide data to Dr. Shen."

"But what if other people see it?" First, the aliens recorded her, now this robot wanted to. What was with everyone trying to turn her into a porn star? Though it would be a great way to pay for college.

"Other people will see it. Dr. Shen will view it many times."

Remy giggled. She bet the horny doc would. She'd probably masturbate watching Remy get rammed by this huge robot. Actually, that was pretty hot, thinking of Sam fingering herself to a sexy video of Remy. She was in!

"Okay, I'm ready to be a porn star!"

T-69 flipped her onto all fours on the table and fucked her doggy style. Its robotic body slapped against her ass as its cock engulfed her tightness.

"Fuck, fuck, fuck!" Remy groaned with every thrust. T-69 was so big, so dominating, so mechanically sexy. What did that mean? She didn't really know, but she apparently had a kink for mechanized lovers.

One of the monitors in the room blipped on. And Remy's ass was front and center. It was a POV shot from the robot's visored head. Its cock rammed into her pussy, her ass cheeks jiggling like gelatin. Fuck, she had no idea how much she liked watching herself get fucked. It made her so fucking wet. And so fucking submissive.

"Oh fuck, T-69, I feel so slutty when you make me watch myself get penetrated!"

"Excellent. This should also help." It snatched her hair with its huge robot hand and tugged her head back. It didn't hurt her, which surprised Remy a little. T-69 was so strong it easily could have. She appreciated that it had a gentle touch when needed.

Another monitor sprang to life, this one featuring a close-up of Remy's face, contorted in sublime, submissive bliss. Shit, there must be other cameras in the room that T-69 could control. It had one on her pussy and ass and one on her face. And Remy couldn't take her eyes off either one. She didn't realize she made such erotic faces when she was being fucked. It's not like she looked at herself in a mirror when she was getting plowed. Though that did sound pretty hot. T-69 was showing her just how wonderfully erotic and submissive she could be.

"Dr. Shen will greatly enjoy the visual contortions of your facial muscles," the robot said.

"Ohhhhh," Remy moaned. "Th... thanks. I think she'll really love this one." Her orgasm hit her hard. Her eyes closed, her mouth opened, and she could only guess how ridiculously slutty her facial expressions were.

Her body convulsed, but T-69 kept her upright. It was far from done with her and had its own cumming to do.

It tugged her hair again. "Look at the monitor while I cum inside you."

"Y… yes, T-69." Remy opened her eyes. She loved that it was ordering her to be so slutty. She watched in awe as it filled her cunt, the sheer volume being so much that some of it spilled back out of her.

It really came spilling out when T-69 removed its dick. She watched the semen pour from her pussy while her robot lover jizzed across her ass.

"Your ass is an excellent size to cum over," it informed her.

"Hey, are you saying I have a big booty?" Remy replied, shaking her tush so she'd get as much cum on it as possible.

"Your posterior is well-proportioned to entice many humans to fondle, spank, and fuck it."

"Oh, well, thanks. That's really sweet of you to say."

"I observe that you have already received many spankings due to the discoloration of your buttocks."

"Oh, yeah, Dr. Shen strapped me to one of her machines and spanked the shit out of me."

"Dr. Shen is very good at spanking sluts."

"She sure is." Remy took no insult at being called a slut. At this point, she was fully on board with being the robot's whore.

"Now it is time to perform another experiment on your ass."

Remy shuddered in T-69's grasp. "You want to fuck me up the butt?"

"Affirmative."

"B… but you're so big. It won't fit."

"That is why it is a good experiment."

Remy gulped. Oh her poor booty.

# Chapter 9

"T-69, could you please fuck my ass with a smaller cock first?" Remy begged. She stared over her shoulder at the robot's ridiculously huge penis that had just dominated her pussy. She had recently discovered she loved ass fuckings but wasn't sure she was ready for such a monstrosity so early in her anal career.

"I am programmed to turn you into a slut. That includes becoming an anal slut."

"Well, if you fuck me in the pussy and ass at the same time, I'll become a really big slut."

"That is logical. Prepare to have both your holes dominated."

Remy trembled. She loved having both her holes dominated.

A second cock emerged from within her metallic lover, smaller than the first but still plenty big to fill her booty.

"You have a lot of nifty gadgets," she told the robot.

"Correct. I have many more to use on you."

Remy trembled even more. How many different decadent toys was T-69 going to subject her to? She hoped a whole bunch!

"Can you lubricate my ass please?" she asked.

"Affirmative. You are a polite human."

"I like being polite when I'm being turned into a slut." Remy tried to be polite all the time, but especially when a sexy robot was dominating her.

"That is logical."

"Thanks!" Remy figured that was a great compliment from a robot. Or from a Vulcan.

"I will use your natural juices to provide lubrication to your posterior."

"There's plenty there to use." Remy was still leaking her own fluids in addition to expelling the robot's cum.

"Yes. You produce a large amount of vaginal juices. That is evidence of how slutty you are."

"Wait, are you saying the more a girl squirts, the bigger a slut she is?"

"That is correct."

"Where did you learn that from?"

"Dr. Shen."

Remy rolled her eyes. That figured. The doc probably loved seeing horny girls squirt. "So I guess I'm pretty slutty then, huh?"

"Extremely. You are an excellent test subject."

"Thanks! Now lube up my ass, please."

T-69 stuck its large index finger partially inside her pussy, moving it up and down and getting it coated in her juices.

Remy wiggled around. The robot's finger was much larger than a human's and felt wonderful tickling her lips.

"I will now penetrate your ass."

Remy appreciated the play-by-play. It made her hornier listening to what T-69 was about to do to her.

The large digit pressed against her tiny opening.

"Uhhhhhh," she groaned as it forced her ass to open and accept the polished probe. A human finger would have been much easier to take, but robot fingers made her feel much sluttier. "Ohhhh, your finger's so big!"

"Your ass is very tiny."

"I thought you said I had a big booty."

"Your overall ass is an ideal size. Your opening is very small, but that is good. It will make you feel every millimeter of my cock." It wiggled its finger inside her, giving her a taste of what its dick would do.

"Ohhh fuck, I need your cock in my ass so bad!"

"Do you feel well lubricated?"

"Oh yeah!"

"Very well. I will penetrate your pussy and ass. But you must be put in a more submissive position." T-69 pushed her head down on the table, keeping her on her knees with her ass sticking up in the air.

Remy gasped. Yup, this was definitely more submissive. With T-69's strong hand between her shoulder blades, she had no chance of moving and had to accept whatever the robot wanted to give her.

It wanted to give her a lot. It entered her pussy and ass. Remy cried out from the dual penetration. One robot cock was amazing. Two were overwhelming.

"Ohhhh fuck, I love robot dicks!"

"That is a natural response." It pressed farther into her. Her pussy and ass were in a perfect position for the robot to fill her deeply.

The cocks completely consumed her. She whimpered and moaned, her hair splayed across her face, her nipples rubbing against the table.

Her pussy and ass throbbed from being so full. T-69 left its appendages fully in her, letting her realize how much control it had over her.

"Do you wish me to initiate the dual fucking?"

"Fuck, yes!"

"That is not the correct response."

"Yes, please?"

"Try again."

Remy grunted. This robot was very particular about how she phrased her requests to be dominated. But it did make her feel more submissive, so it knew what it was doing.

"Please fuck both my slutholes and turn me into the biggest whore on the planet!"

"That is acceptable."

Remy sighed. Thank goodness. She was getting antsy about getting rammed.

T-69 thrust its hips back and forth, pummeling her two holes. The sounds of its metal gears mixed with the squishing of her pussy and ass.

"Ohhhhh, you're fucking me so hard!"

"That is my mission."

"You have an awesome mission!"

"I will not rest until all women become robot sluts." It increased its fucking speed. Remy screamed in pleasure. Dammit, this robot knew how to fuck. But did it really intend to turn every woman into a slut? Was this how AI would take over the world? It certainly was taking over Remy's pussy and ass, and Remy was more than happy to let it. The way T-69 was pounding her, she was fine becoming a sex slave to artificial lifeforms.

"I'll be your first slut!" she confessed.

"Good. Now increase the decibels of your vocal sluttiness while I pound you."

Remy complied, moaning loudly as T-69 fucked her pussy and ass like it owned them. She was glad the strip mall was mostly abandoned. Otherwise, everyone would know what a vocal whore she was. She imagined the blinds opening and a bevy of onlookers ogling her naked body as she got smashed by a sex robot. That was hot. Maybe she should scream even louder to encourage any passers-by to come in.

"I will now fill both your holes. You will take all my cum like a good whore."

"Ohhhhh, yes! Give me all your cum! I promise I'll keep it

in me and won't let it out until you say I can."

"Good. You are becoming a proper slut." T-69 unleashed its creamy cum from both cocks, flooding Remy's holes.

"Ohhh fuck, so much cum!" She squirmed around, wondering if she could contain her lover's fake semen.

She couldn't. It filled her so much, the white fluids poured out of her and dripped onto the table between her legs.

"You promised to accept all my cum," the robot chided her.

"I'm sorry! My pussy and ass are too tiny for your robot stickiness!"

"That is no excuse."

"Aw, c'mon, can't I make it up to you?"

"Yes. You can become much sluttier."

"Okay!" Remy found herself wanting to please the horny robot. "How do I do that?"

"By performing oral sex on both my robotic cocks."

Remy gasped. She had never given a blowjob to a robot before. Of course, until last night, she had never sucked off aliens either. Like all good sci-fi loving girls, she knew it was important not to discriminate against different species or artificial entities. So it was her duty as a human to show this robot she had no problem going down on it. "I will happily suck your robot cocks!"

"Very good. You are an accommodating human."

Remy nodded. She hoped that would go a long way to her surviving the AI apocalypse.

But she couldn't give T-69 oral with it holding her down on the table. "Um, could you let me up so I can deep throat you?"

"Yes. But first I must apply these magnetic restraints." It slapped two bronze bracelets on her wrists, which were immediately pulled together and bound behind her back.

"Oh my goodness, what are those?"

"They are restraints that will allow me to bind you to anything metallic. You will perform fellatio on me with your arms bound behind your back."

Remy raised her head up. "Wow, you're a very commanding robot."

"Affirmative. I must be in order to create multitudes of sluts."

"Well, I appreciate you taking your job so seriously."

"It is important work."

Remy giggled. She supposed creating sluts was important.

"Did I utter an amusing remark?"

"No. Well, sort of. We humans just like to giggle sometimes."

"You are a strange species. But one that is enjoyable to fuck."

"Yes! We're very fuckable." Remy was liking this robot more and more. Maybe she could teach it about humanity while it was slutting her up.

"Now, attend to my cocks."

Remy knew not to disobey, not that she wanted to. She had been staring at the dual robot cocks, excited to take them in her mouth.

"I will initiate self-cleaning mode to make my cocks fresh for you." Soapy suds covered its dicks, followed by a spray of water. The cocks gleamed before her, ready to be swallowed.

"Thanks! You're a very considerate robot."

"You are welcome. But remember, my main consideration is to turn you into a slut."

"Right. I haven't forgotten. I feel I am well on my way to becoming your whore."

"That is welcome news. Now, initiate oral."

Remy initiated oral. She started with his smaller cock,

wrapping her lips around it. It was harder than a human penis but still had a fleshy texture to it.

She sucked him for a few minutes, then pulled back, gazing up at him. "How's that so far?"

"My sensors estimate that your oral skills are mediocre."

"What?!"

"You must do better to initiate my orgasmic sequence."

"You're saying I give bad blowjobs?" Remy pouted, furious that the robot had insulted her oral skills. She thought she was pretty good at sucking dick.

"I did not say that. I said you were average."

"I don't want to be average. I want to be amazing!"

"Then cease your human pouting and get back to work."

"Fine," she harrumphed, muttering under her breath that the aliens didn't have any complaints. Of course, she couldn't understand the aliens. But they all came down her throat, so they must have enjoyed it. Dammit, she would have to find those five alien hotties again and figure out a way to communicate so she could know for sure if they enjoyed her mouth.

T-69 snatched her hair and shoved her onto its cock, making her take the entire thing.

"Mmrph!" she said with a mouth full of robot penis.

"I will assist you in feeling slutty by forcing you to take my penis."

Remy tried to say "thank you" but it was hard with a dick in her mouth. The robot thrust her head back and forth, making her take his entire shaft each time. She pursed her lips, tightening them around his cock as much as she could.

T-69 paused after many thrusts. "Use your tongue. That will increase my desire to climax."

Remy flicked her tongue across the tip of its cock, tasting the robotic pre-cum.

"That is very good. Your prowess at oral stimulation is increasing rapidly."

Remy went back to sucking. Yes! She was redeeming herself. She wasn't sure why the robot's opinion of her was so important. She wasn't developing feelings for it, was she? Maybe she just knew it was an expert on all things sexual and figured she could gain tips on how to please lovers: robot, human, and alien.

"Excellent suction. You will soon make me cum."

Remy squealed through his penis. She was becoming a cock-sucking queen!

The robot cock expanded and unleashed its cum. It held Remy's mouth on its dick, making sure she gulped down every last drop it had to give.

And it had a lot to give. It gushed down her throat. She had to swallow rapidly to keep up with the flow.

"Continue drinking," it ordered. "I have much more to release."

Remy stared up at its faceless head, guzzling its cum while she perched on the table on her knees with her arms bound behind her. This robot wasn't kidding when it said it would turn her into a slut. She felt so fucking submissive, so under the robot's power. And she fucking loved it!

Remy didn't know how much cum she drank, but when it finally pulled out of her mouth, she gasped for air. It shot the rest of its semen across her tits, leaving them stained with white streaks.

She panted, her breasts heaving. "Okay, I did a good job, right? And don't say I was just mediocre."

"You scored very high on the robot fellatio scale."

"There's a robot fellatio scale?"

"Of course. There is a robot scale for everything. It is extremely accurate. Infallible even."

Remy rolled her eyes. Robots could be kind of arrogant. But she still liked them.

"Well, I'm glad I got a high score. Grades are really important to me."

"It is logical for you to want to do well in school. I will ensure you receive high grades in sluttiness."

"Yay! Thanks, T-69!" Wait, why was she so excited about that? Academic grades were always important to her, and she excelled in school. But since when did slutty grades become so important? And since when did robots hand out slutty grades? It was all the fault of those aliens. They had really showed her the huge appeal of being a kinky slut!

"To receive an A, you must now suck my larger cock."

Remy stared at the monstrosity before her. It was so much bigger than the penis she had just sucked.

How on earth was she going to fit it in her mouth? And how much more cum was it going to expel compared to its little brother?

Looked like Remy was about to find out.

# Chapter 10

Remy examined the robot cock from all angles.

"Are you analyzing my appendage?" T-69 asked.

"Yup. I'm trying to figure out how to fit it in my mouth."

"I will fuck your pussy to motivate you."

"Good idea!"

The robot's arm extended down until it reached Remy's dripping cunt. It inserted a finger inside her, the digit growing in length and girth until it completely filled her.

"Ohhhh fuck, I'm really getting motivated!" Remy wailed.

"Good. Now take my dick in your mouth."

Remy placed her lips around T-69's bulbous head, sucking on it gently. She figured she'd tease her mechanical lover a bit and also give herself time to adjust to the huge monstrosity.

"That is good, but you must take it farther in your mouth." It vibrated its finger in her pussy, making her squeal and providing her with plenty of impetus to give it a more proper mouth fucking.

Remy inched forward, taking more of its shaft.

"Do you feel like a slut?" T-69 asked.

"Mmm hrmph," Remy said. It was hard to talk with a big robot dick in your mouth.

"Then you should take more of it."

Remy's eyes widened. This robot was so commanding. It was determined to make Remy do any sexual thing it wanted. Of course, so far, Remy had no issue satisfying its kinky requests. The more it demanded of her, the more she wanted to please it.

T-69 vibrated her pussy more powerfully. Remy began leaking more juices, which made her want to take as much of the robot's cock as she could. It was only fair for her to provide it with intense pleasure too.

She took its cock until she gagged on it, then pulled back a bit, finding a comfortable spot to fully fuck it.

She gave her robot lover a deep, sexy blowjob, while it gave her a deep, sexy fingering.

"You are activating my pleasure sensors. You are very talented at satisfying robot cocks."

Remy sucked harder. She was happy to get the robot stamp of approval for her fellatio skills.

"You are going to make me cum down your throat," it informed her. It was a little strange to hear someone announce they were about to cum in such a monotone voice. But she supposed it was a very normal thing for robots.

She would have screamed "Please cum down my throat!" but that would have entailed taking the penis out of her mouth, and she didn't want to miss any of T-69's juicy jizz. Its artificial semen tasted sweeter than real cum, so she was more than happy to gulp it down. Plus, she knew T-69 wouldn't be happy if she didn't take everything it wanted to give. She needed to show her lover she was a good submissive slut.

The robot unloaded on her, making a weird robot grunt as its creamy liquid flowed down her throat. It grabbed her head with its other hand, making sure she kept her mouth around its quivering penis and drank every last drop of its cum.

But it also made sure she had a fantastic orgasm, vibrating her pussy so hard she spewed all over the table, which had gotten so wet from all her squirting, she didn't know if Dr. Shen would ever get it fully clean.

T-69 filled her with its cum then pulled out, holding its cock above her. "Present your tits so I may coat them properly."

Remy thrust her boobs out, which was easy to do with her arms tied behind her.

Her lover came all over them, a thick layer of semen hardening over her fleshy mounds.

"Oh my goodness, I've never seen anyone who can cum as much as you," she remarked.

"Robots are excellent at cumming," it agreed. "Though your ability nearly rivals mine. You make for an excellent slutty test subject."

"Um, thanks. I'm learning a lot about how much I can shoot my girl juices."

"That is an excellent education."

Remy giggled. The robot made it sound like the real reason to go to college was to learn how to be slutty and have amazing orgasms. Well, she had to admit it was more fun than studying, even though she enjoyed her academic courses. "Do you have more ways to educate me?"

"Of course." It affixed circular restraints around her ankles, similar to the ones around her wrists.

"Oh, so now you can control my arms and legs?"

"Correct. Sluts should be helpless to their robot masters."

Remy gulped. Oh man, this was getting kinky. Did it

expect her to call it "Master?" Would she have to call Dr. Shen "Mistress?" That actually might be hot.

T-69 lifted her off the table, turned her around, and used the magnetic pull of its body to yank her arms and legs against it. She wound up plastered to the robot's frame, spreadeagle, with its cocks directly below her pussy.

Remy pulled against her restraints, but they wouldn't budge. Crap, she was basically fused to T-69's body, where it could carry her around like she was a doll. A sex doll in this case. How did this robot keep coming up with ways to make her feel more and more submissive? Oh right, it was programmed to do that. Dr. Shen was a dangerous woman. She could turn any woman into a huge slut with her crazy inventions.

But right now, Remy was thrilled the doc was so talented. She loved being at the mercy of T-69 and couldn't wait to see what it was going to do to her next.

"I detect your body heat increasing. That indicates you are becoming more aroused."

"Um, yup."

"Why are you becoming more aroused?"

"B... because I'm completely helpless and you can do

whatever you want to me."

"State what you feel like."

"I... like a slutty sex toy."

"Correct. You are learning. You stated the correct answer on the first try."

Remy smiled. Yes! She was learning the right slutty sayings. Wait, was that really a good thing? Heck yeah it was! Saying slutty stuff meant her lovers would fuck her even harder and make her cum even more spectacularly.

"So, um, what are you going to do me now?"

"I will place a vibrating device against your clit and make you cum non-stop."

"That sounds amazing!"

"Yes. We will do it for at least an hour."

"What?! You're going to make me cum non-stop for an hour?"

"Of course."

"I can't cum that much!"

"Your cumming ability has proven more than up to the task so far."

Remy blushed. "Oh, um, thanks. But if I do it for that long, I think I'll pass out."

"Do not concern yourself. If you do, I will keep you safe and replenish you with fluids."

"Really?"

"Of course. One of my missions is to protect you."

"It is? I thought it was to turn me into a slut."

"Yes. But I must protect all my sluts. I will not let any harm befall you."

Remy's heart melted. "Oh T-69, that's so sweet. I'd kiss you, but I can't really reach you in the position I'm in."

"You may bestow your human affection upon me later."

Remy smiled, wondering if the robot was looking forward to getting smooched. It had probably never been kissed before. Remy could be the first girl to kiss this sex robot. She'd be famous if she kept having all these sexy firsts with aliens, robots, and who knew what else.

T-69's dual dicks retracted into its body, replaced by a smaller device that hovered over Remy's clit. It vibrated her nub softly, easily getting it to pop out of its hood. It then produced a small suction cup, which latched on to her clit, completely encircling it.

"Yikes! You've captured my clit!" It wasn't quite the same as "You've captured my battleship," but it was way sexier.

"Affirmative. Your clit now belongs to me."

"O... okay." Remy couldn't think of a good reason why the robot shouldn't own her clit.

The device sucked and vibrated her most sensitive spot in ways Remy didn't know were possible.

"Holy fucking shiiiiiittttttt!" Her body convulsed against T-69, her ass banging against its firm frame. It took less than two seconds for the robot to make her cum. It shot straight out of her, a huge single spray that splattered against the floor.

Her mechanical master alternated suction and speed, making her alternate from single streams to wide sprays. She had never had anyone control the way she came as much as T-69.

"Ohhhhhhh fuck! H... how are you controlling my squirting like this?"

"I am very skilled in controlling slutty pussies."

"You sure are!" She sent another blast across her and T-69's legs. "I... I hope you're waterproof."

"Yes. I am fully water resistant. Feel free to cum as much as you want."

"Th... thanks!" Remy didn't have much of a choice. T-69's manipulations of her clit had her waterworks turned on full with no end in sight.

Orgasm after orgasm overwhelmed her. She couldn't move her arms or legs thanks to T-69's magnets holding her in place. All she could do is thrash around and gush gallons of her cum.

She passed out. Woke up. Came a bunch more. Passed out again.

When she came to, a straw hovered below her lips.

"Drink," T-69 told her. "You must replenish your fluids."

She eagerly took the plastic tube in her mouth and sucked up the water flowing from a small hole in the robot's faceplate. It was handy that it had reservoirs of both water and cum.

She drank at least half a liter, then let out a contented sigh.

"How do you feel?" T-69 asked.

"Much better. Thank you. You're a nice robot."

"I… am not sure how to reply to that."

"It's a compliment. Just say 'thank you.'"

"Very well. Thank you."

"You're welcome. I see I'm still attached to you." She remained bound to the robot, limbs splayed.

"Of course. You are my sex toy."

"You're definitely making me feel like one."

"Good. I am fulfilling my mission."

Remy sipped more water. "Yup. So are you getting good data for Dr. Shen?"

"Affirmative. You are an ideal test subject. Dr. Shen chose wisely."

Remy smiled. She didn't realize she had such natural skills as a fuck toy. She had learned a lot about herself in the past two days.

"So what can your sex toy do for you next?"

"We must make you more submissive."

"More?! But I'm already doing everything you command."

"That is good. But we must push your sluttiness to its limits."

"We must?"

"Affirmative."

"Well, okay." Remy knew no self-respecting geek girl would turn down additional fun times with a sex robot. These opportunities didn't come around every day. She needed to milk this for all it was worth. And then T-69 could milk her pussy. Wait, did that make sense? Not really, but, hey, it was hard to think straight after being fucked non-stop by a sex robot.

"I am glad you confirm you should become sluttier. I shall now fuck you in public."

"Sounds go… what?!!!" It took Remy a second to process what it just said. "You're going to fuck me where other people can see?"

"Of course. All true sluts are exhibitionists."

Remy shivered. Where was this kooky robot getting its information? She didn't think all sluts necessarily liked performing in public. What was wrong with being a private slut? Remy was getting really good at that.

"Commencing public slut program."

It marched toward the windows.

Remy gulped. Oh fuck, what had she gotten herself into?

# Chapter 11

The blinds on the windows rose, the afternoon sunlight streaming in.

T-69 plastered Remy's body against the glass, her tits creating steamy circles. She was still attached to her robot master by the magnetic restraints and could do nothing to prevent her naked body being shown to the world.

"Ahh! T-69, you're showing my tits to everyone!"

"There is no one in the parking lot," it responded.

"But someone might walk by."

"Unlikely. All the neighboring storefronts have been closed for years. The only open businesses are 152 meters away."

Remy gazed out the window. She knew what T-69 said was true, but the fact that her naked assets were being presented to the outside world made her nervous. It also made her hot. Her pussy had that pleasant warm feeling it always did when she got turned on.

"However," the robot continued. "If you would like, I will alert the local news outlets that there is a bound slut at this location begging to be photographed and videoed."

"Ack! Don't do that! It'd be so embarrassing!" The last thing Remy needed was for her parents to see her totally naked and being fucked by a sex robot on the evening news. Even though the thought of people taking pictures of T-69 dominating her did excite her.

"Do not worry. I was merely joshing. Dr. Shen says I should work on my robot humor."

Remy breathed a sigh of relief. Her naked tits were safe for the moment. And she was learning more about her robotic paramour. Who knew it had a sense of humor? "Oh, well, that's good, but your jokes need some work."

"I will continue working on my humor until I have mastered human comedy."

"Great! But, um, will all your jokes be about my naked body?"

"There is a strong likelihood of that. You must always be naked when you are in my presence."

"Wait? I can't ever wear clothes around you."

"Sluts do not wear clothing around their robot

dominators."

Remy sighed. Guess she was going to be naked a whole bunch. What was with all these non-human creatures wanting her to be super-nude? First the aliens, now this robot. She might as well donate all her clothes to charity. Of course, it was flattering that aliens and robots desired her nude flesh so much. She liked that she was so popular with sci-fi creatures.

"Well, I guess that makes sense," she told T-69. "I suppose robots are always quite logical."

"Of course. The most logical thing is to turn beautiful women into sluts."

Remy giggled. Only a robot programmed by Dr. Shen would cite that logic. "Aw, you think I'm beautiful?"

"Yes. My data on human ideals of beauty place you in the top five percent of women."

Remy blushed. That was crazy flattering. "N… no way."

"Yes way."

Remy smiled. "That's the nicest thing anyone's ever said to me. Thanks, T-69!"

"You are welcome, my beautiful slut."

Remy shivered. Oh wow, she liked having a robot call her a beautiful slut. It was sweet and saucy and made her tingle all over.

"Oh God, you're making me so wet when you say things like that. Please fuck me against the glass and make me an exhibitionist!" Remy's reservations about being fucked in public were quickly evaporating. Her robot lover had a way of making her crave new experiences. Dr. Shen had programmed it well.

"Affirmative. I will fuck you until you cover the glass with your juices." Its legs extended so Remy's pussy was also visible through the window. Apparently, it wasn't content with her providing a peep show with only her tits.

Its huge cock emerged from its body and slid upward into Remy's waiting pussy.

"Uhhhhhh!" she moaned. "Fuck, you're so big!"

"Do you enjoy big cocks?" it asked as it inserted the phallic monstrosity all the way inside her.

"Oh God, I love them!"

"Good. Then I will ram your pussy at extremely high velocity." The robot cock moved up and down like a jackhammer, pummeling Remy's pussy like it was drilling for oil, or in this case, Remy's sweet nectar.

"Oh myyyyy fuckkkkinnnnng Godddddddddd!!!" T-69's

pounding was so intense, Remy felt like her pussy was going to be destroyed by the robot cock. But destroyed in the best way possible. Her entire body writhed and bounced against the glass, the huge jackhammer jizzmaster sending vibrations all the way to her extremities.

"Do you enjoy having your pussy pounded by a robot cock?" T-69 asked.

"Y… yes!"

"Do you enjoy being helpless and fucked in front of a window?"

"God, yes!"

"Do you consent to being my whore and letting me fuck you wherever I deem fit?"

"Yes, fuck, yes! You can fuck me anytime and anywhere you want!" Remy knew she might regret saying that. T-69 likely had some very kinky places it wanted to fuck her. But in the moment, she didn't care. Her pleasure sensors were overloaded and easily overrode her brain's logic.

"Those are excellent answers. I will now make you cum."

"Ohhhh yes! Please make me cum, T-69!" She wanted it so bad. She didn't care if anyone came by and saw her. They should know what a huge, sci-fi slut she was.

T-69 attached its suction cup to her clit, sucking on her most sensitive spot while continuing to pound her pussy.

Remy shook like she was having a seizure. Getting her pussy fucked at such extreme speed and her clit sucked so hard was almost too much to bear. She knew an overpowering orgasm was imminent.

And that's when a homeless man pushed a shopping cart by the window. He stooped to collect a bottle, his back to Remy.

Remy's eyes went wide. Holy shit, if he turned around, he'd totally see her. See her naked, bound, and fucked by a robot, about to cum all over the place. She knew being a kinky exhibitionist would bite her in the ass. Which is the one thing no one had done to her lately, even though they had done pretty much everything else to her juicy butt.

Her voice was lost to throaty moans from T-69's expert fucking, so she couldn't ask her strong lover to move her away from the window. And she wasn't sure she would even if she could find her voice. Something about being so close to being caught in the act thrilled her. It made her want it more, want to be turned into a slut in front of an audience.

That part of her got her wish. The man picked up another

bottle right below the window then raised his head, his eyes trailing up Remy's naked, bound body.

He dropped the bottle and stared at her slack-jawed, watching her pussy and tits slide up and down the window, gaping at the ridiculously huge robot cock filling her.

She tried to smile but wound up making sex faces at him. It was hard to do much else with how T-69 was fucking her. Her robot companion didn't seem bothered in the least by the surprise voyeur. It probably thought having an audience would make her even sluttier.

She managed to wiggle her fingers and wave at the man. While it was an extremely embarrassing situation, there was no reason she couldn't be polite.

He waved back, a huge smile on his face. Well, at least she was making a lot of people happy lately: this guy, the aliens, Dr. Shen, and T-69.

"Ohhhhhh," she cried. "I'm going to cum right in front of him!"

"That is good," her machine lover replied. "Show him what a good slut you are."

"O... okay." She showed the lucky guy what a good slut she was by making the most erotic orgasmic faces ever and squirting all over the window. Her liquid splashed off it and soaked her thighs, while the rest spilled down the glass in large streaks.

The man's jaw dropped. He stared in awe at the sheer volume coming out of Remy's cunt.

"I… I think he's really enjoying it!" she screamed.

"Yes. I am sure he has never seen a whore eject so much fluid before."

"Ahhhh! When you call me a whore, you just make me cum more!"

"That is why I will continue to call you that."

"Okay, great!" Remy splattered a bunch more of her goodness against the glass, glad her robot master would continue to call her naughty names.

T-69 took a step back and rotated her body back and forth. Her juices continued to shoot out like a squirt gun, spraying the entirety of the windows.

"Ohhhhhh God, w… what are you doing?"

"Using your cum to clean the glass. You are an excellent window washer." It continued to twist its body, using her pussy like it was a bottle of glass cleaner.

"Ohhhhh! Is… is that another one of your robot jokes?"

"Yes. But it is also intended to make you feel like a sex toy. Is it working?"

"Fuck, yes! I've never felt so submissive in my life!" While the aliens had made Remy feel crazy submissive, T-69 was literally using her pussy as a tool, which drove her wild with the desire to be subservient.

"Good. I am glad my programming is proving to be effective."

"Ohhhhh! S... so effective!"

The man outside pressed his face to the glass, trying to see through the cum coating. Remy had covered the entire window by now, making it very difficult to see inside.

T-69 turned around, the blinds lowering behind them. Remy surmised it could control them remotely, as it likely could many things in the room.

"G... guess the peep show is over," she said breathlessly, more glops of her cum dripping out of her while T-69 marched across the room.

"For now. But do not worry. I will fuck you more publicly soon."

Remy trembled. She wasn't sure if she wanted to protest or encourage her metallic lover. While mortifying, it was pretty thrilling being helpless and forced to cum in front of the man outside. She wondered if he'd tell his friends he saw a young slut being fucked out of her mind by a sex robot. Probably not. Who would believe him? Even Remy couldn't believe all the crazy stuff that had happened to her over the past two days. Somehow she had become a sex magnet to everything weird and kinky. Lucky her!

T-69 detached her from its body and spun her around so she was facing it. It sat on a reinforced chair, lowering her so she straddled its lap, its cock once again penetrating her pussy.

"Ohhhh fuck!" Every time it entered her, she couldn't help squealing. Its cock was that amazing.

"You may rest before I continue fucking you."

"Th... thanks. But do I need to rest with your cock in my pussy?"

"Of course." It didn't elaborate. Evidently, T-69 thought it was obvious sluts would rest with their lover's cock filling them. She couldn't fault its logic.

"Oh, okay." Remy rested her head and hands against T-69's chest, closing her eyes and feeling the warmth of her robot lover. Even though its body was normally cool, it was able to generate a pleasing heat throughout its chest and dick, making Remy feel nice and toasty.

"This is cozy," she sighed. "Put your arms around me."

"Why should I take that action?"

"Because it's romantic, silly."

"I am programmed for sex, not romance."

"But you can learn new things, right?"

"Affirmative."

"Okay, well, after fucking a girl's brains out, it's nice to cuddle with her."

"What is cuddling?"

"You know, hugging, nuzzling noses, kissing."

"I do not have a nose to nuzzle or a mouth to kiss."

"That's okay. I can nuzzle and kiss you. But only if you put your arms around me."

"Very well." It encircled her back, squeezing with just the right amount of pressure. Remy had been impressed by how it had never hurt her even with how strong it was.

"That's it! You're a good hugger. Now, for your kisses." She smooched its chestplate and nuzzled her nose against it. It wasn't the same as a human chest, but it was still kind of nice.

"You seem to be an affectionate human."

"Yup. At least with people and robots I like."

"You *like* me?"

"Sure."

"Even though I have ordered you to be a slut."

"Oh yeah. I like being slutty for sexy robots."

It seemed to process that for a moment. "You are an intelligent woman."

Remy smiled. "Thank you!"

T-69's cock expanded inside her, making her wiggle on its lap. Was her sweetness turning it on? Could it learn to have feelings for her? Remy was becoming more and more interested in spending time with this kinky construction. Maybe it could provide romance and amazing sex: a sci-fi nerd's dream come true!

Before she could ponder that further, the door to the room opened.

She froze. Oh no, did the man outside tell everyone in the nearby shops to come see the robot slut in the window? Would she have to put on a sex show and let T-69 dominate her in front of everyone?

She gulped. She might have to take her exhibitionism to the next level.

# Chapter 12

Dr. Shen strolled in, slurping a strawberry smoothie. "Oh good, you're on T-69's cock."

"Yup," Remy replied. "I've been on it virtually the whole time you've been gone."

"Excellent! Has Remy been a good girl for you, T-69?"

"Affirmative. She has performed like a true slut and taken my cocks in her pussy and ass."

Remy blushed. "Ahh, T-69, you don't have to be so blunt about it."

"Do you dispute the veracity of my statements?"

"Um, no. It's just… I'm embarrassed I was so slutty!"

"Don't be embarrassed," Sam said, slurping more loudly. "You should be proud."

"Indeed," her robot creation added. "All women should aspire to be huge sluts."

Remy rolled her eyes. "You've created a very kinky robot."

"What other kind is there?" Sam replied. "Now, tell me

everything T-69 did to you, and don't leave out any details." She hopped on a stool and opened her laptop.

Remy's mind raced through all the ridiculously submissive things her robot lover made her do. "Um, well, he fucked me a whole bunch, I squirted all over the place, the end."

"What?! That was no details at all. T-69, remind her what a whore she is."

"As you wish." The mechanical pussy master vibrated its cock inside Remy, making her cum instantly.

"Ohhhhh fuck! I'm cumming so hard!" Remy squirted past her favorite dick, her hips squirming on T-69's lap, her ass cheeks shaking sensually.

T-69 grabbed her ass firmly. "Tell the doctor what she wishes to hear."

"Ohhhhh! Y... yes, T-69." Remy couldn't refuse her lover when it squeezed her ass like that. Or when it make her cum so spectacularly.

She regaled Sam with all the ways T-69 had fucked her, her cheeks turning redder and redder as she got to each submissive story.

Dr. Shen's fingers flew across the keyboard, noting every kinky detail. Remy blushed even more, knowing that all her slutty behavior was being saved for posterity. But it also made her pussy burn with the desire to be fucked over and over again by her robot master.

"Wow," Sam remarked after she finished her notes. "That's super-hot you fucked her against the glass. Good thinking, T-69."

"That seemed to make her particularly slutty. Especially when the human male was watching."

Remy trembled on the robot's cock, picturing how helpless she was being fucked against the window, cumming like a whore for the lucky guy outside.

Sam raised her hands. "Yes! My invention's working even better than I expected. Thanks for being my test subject!"

"S… sure. It was fun. Even though you were sneaky and left me at T-69's mercy."

"Sorry! But the meeting was really important."

"Was it really important you stop to get a smoothie on the way back?"

Sam glanced at her drink. "Oops. Okay, maybe I should have hurried back sooner. But these smoothies are soooo good. Here, try some." She shoved the straw in Remy's mouth. The young slut sipped it eagerly. All that fucking made her very thirsty.

"Mmm, that is good. Why didn't you get me one?"

"Um, double oops? Honestly, I thought you'd be passed out from all the intense fucking T-69 gave you. I'm impressed you took all that. You must be a super-slut!"

"Hey! I'm not a super-slut."

T-69 rumbled within her and made her cum again.

"Ohhhhhhh fuck! Okay, I'm a super-slut!"

Sam smiled. "T-69 can be very convincing."

Remy nodded. "Soooo convincing."

"Okay, I have a bunch of questions to ask you about how slutty you felt during each fucking." The hot doc poised her fingers over the laptop again.

T-69 slammed it shut and set it on a counter.

"T-69, what are you doing?" Sam asked in shock.

"Before you ask your questions, Dr. Shen, I must fulfill my mission."

"But you've already turned Remy into a slut."

Remy scrunched up her nose. She was being called a slut an awful lot today. But she supposed letting five aliens and a robot ravage her qualified as pretty slutty behavior.

"My mission is to turn all women into sluts," the robot

informed Sam. "That includes you."

"What?!"

Remy's eyes widened. Oh shit, the sexy doc was about to get a taste of her own medicine. Remy couldn't wait to see this.

Sam fidgeted on the stool. "But I'm the scientist. I need to record the data on other sluts."

"Do not worry. I will video everything so you can make a detailed report afterwards."

"But that will be so embarrassing!"

"Hey!" Remy protested. "You had T-69 video me."

"That's different."

"How?"

"I like watching sexy girls get fucked by robots."

Remy rolled her eyes. What a kooky mad scientist. "Well, so do I!"

"Oh. That's a fair point."

T-69 had grown tired of their chatting. He ripped Sam's clothes off, while keeping Remy impaled on his cock.

"Eek! I'm naked!" Sam hopped from one foot to the other, trying to figure out if she should cover up or flaunt her goodies.

Remy was happy to see her new friend went for the flaunting option. The psychologist had cute, firm breasts and enough curves in her hips to prove geeky scientists could be super-sexy. As a lover of all things geeky, Remy had a serious weak spot for sexy, nerdy girls. She wanted to high five T-69 for showing her his creator's assets. She also wanted to put her hands all over those assets, especially Sam's ridiculously tiny vagina with its shaved, bare lips on display.

"Oh my God, you're so sexy!" Remy squealed.

Sam stopped fidgeting. "I am?"

"Of course, silly. I want to fuck you so bad!" Remy gasped. "Oops, did I say that out loud?"

"Affirmative," T-69 helpfully told her.

"You can totally fuck me!" Sam replied.

"I will be fucking both of you first," the robot informed them.

Remy wiggled on his lap. "I thought you were going to fuck Sam."

"I am. But I must make sure you do not forget what a huge slut you are."

"I don't think I'm going to forget." There was no way she could, not after all the ways T-69 had dominated her.

"Good. But there is no reason to take any chances."

"You're probably right," Remy agreed. She wasn't going to turn down more AI fucking.

"Robots are always right."

Sam bit her lip. "Yikes! I think I might have programmed it too well."

Remy nodded. "I think you did. But, oh well, let's get fucked!"

T-69 threw them both on a nearby couch, Sam on her back, Remy lying face first on top of her. The cute doc's nipples rubbed against Remy's, igniting them into action.

"Oh God, you have amazing tits!" Remy cried.

"So do you!" Sam echoed. She threw her arms around Remy and brought her in closer, making their nipples do some dirty dancing.

"Good," T-69 said, appreciating their slutty behavior. "You should manipulate each other's breasts while I fuck you."

Remy glanced over her shoulder. Four cocks emerged from the robot's body: two big, two small. Well, to be more exact: two huge, two not quite-as-huge. "You're going to fuck all four of our holes at once?"

"Of course. You should be aware by now that sluts love to

be fucked in the pussy and ass."

"Oh, right. Silly me, I forgot."

"Do not worry. I will remind you most vigorously."

Remy shivered. She loved robot reminders like that.

The robot straddled them and aimed its quadruple cocks at their tight holes.

Remy's pussy and ass were pierced simultaneously. "Ohhhh fuccckkkk!" There was nothing quite like getting a dual penetration. It made her whole body tremble, her pussy and ass wracked by sinful sensations.

"Ohh God, they're so big!" Sam wailed. Unlike Remy, she hadn't gotten as much practice with T-69's behemoths. Remy knew exactly what it felt like to get that first taste of robot cock.

She brushed the sexy doc's cheeks with her fingers. "It's okay, just look at me, I've got you. It will get easier the more it fucks you."

Sam gazed at Remy gratefully. "O… okay."

T-69 examined the proximity of the women's faces. "That is a good idea. You should kiss while I fuck you." It forced its cocks in deeper, making both of them squeal.

Sam opened her mouth and scrunched her nose up in one

of the cutest sex faces Remy had ever seen. "Oh fuck, yes! Please kiss me! You're so fucking hot!"

Remy smiled. She was starting to really like this horny scientist. She pressed her lips against Sam's, more than happy to smooch the beautiful Chinese woman. The sex psychologist's lips were like jasmine and honey, and Remy quickly fell into a deep kiss with her. Sam kissed Remy just as eagerly, their intimate embrace helping them take the full length of all of T-69's cocks.

"I am now fully inside you," it helpfully informed them.

Remy and Sam moaned their assent into each others' mouths.

"I will begin fucking you roughly. Continue kissing each other unless I command you to utter something slutty."

"Y... yes, T-69!" Remy cried, momentarily removing her lips from Sam's.

"We'll do whatever you say!" Sam added. Remy went back to kissing her, realizing they had pretty much become the robot's sex slaves. T-69 had made two girls its fuck toys in record time. This was one skilled robot.

Their mechanical master smashed all four cocks into their pussies and asses. The girls' bodies rubbed back and forth against each other. They clung to each other for dear life, kissing and moaning and feeling like huge sluts.

Remy's pussy and ass were ridiculously full. But kissing Sam made it easier to take. The sexy scientist's lips were so wonderful, her body so soft and inviting, Remy hoped their robot lover would force them to make out every time it fucked them.

"Remy, do you feel like a robot fuck toy?" it asked.

"Oh fuck, yes! I'm absolutely your fuck toy, T-69!"

"Excellent. Dr. Shen, please admit that you are a sex slave to robots."

"Ohhhhh! Yes! I love being your sex slave! I'll be a sex slave to all robots!"

"Me too!" Remy agreed.

"Very good. You are the perfect test subjects. I will now make you cum all over each other."

Remy spasmed. Yes! She so wanted to cum on Sam. The only thing that would make the Asian beauty's body hotter was Remy's juices all over it. And she would happily take all of Sam's pussy juice.

T-69 jackhammered them, four holes pounded as deeply as possible, until their pussies erupted.

"Ohhhhhhh God, I'm cumming!" Remy screamed.

"Me tooooooooo!" Sam screamed just as loudly.

T-69 removed its cocks from their pussies, letting them freely squirt. And boy did they. They soaked each others' thighs, trying to hang on to each other as their bodies convulsed out of control.

T-69 continued to fuck their asses, making sure they had plenty of motivation to continue to cum.

"I… I can't stop cumming!" Remy confessed.

"Me either!!"

"That is good. You will not stop until I state that you can." T-69 placed two vibrating fingers on their clits, making them erupt even harder.

"Fuuuuuuucccccckkkkkkk!!!" the two girls shrieked, their wet, naked bodies gyrating against each other.

They kept cumming. And cumming. And cumming. They had no way to stop with what T-69 was doing to their clits and asses. Their robot overlord had taken command of their orgasms. Remy had never felt this much under someone's power before. She was glad Sam was here with her. If she was going to be a robot sex toy, it was nice to have a fellow sexy slut with her.

"You may stop cumming." It pulled its ass cocks out of them, and gave them one last jolt from its fingers. They shot out two final streams, then collapsed against each other, panting and sweating.

"Holy shit, that was amazing!" Sam gasped.

"Uh huh. Now you know what I've been experiencing ever since you left."

"You lucky slut!"

Remy smiled. She supposed she was lucky. She was the first girl to get slutted up by T-69. "You're a really good kisser," she told the hot doc underneath her.

"I could kiss you all day long!" Sam replied.

"I won't say no to that!" Remy was eager to smooch her a bunch more.

T-69 lifted them off the couch. "Before you do that, I must fuck you again."

Remy patted the robot's arm. "Okay, where do you want us this time, T-69?" She was in no position to refuse, nor did she want to.

"Outside. On your vehicle's hood."

"What?!!" both women said in shock.

Remy clutched its huge robot bicep. "But you already

fucked me against the open window. Wasn't that enough of a public slut display?"

"No. You must be fucked fully in public to be a true whore."

Remy turned to Sam. "What kind of wacky rules did you program it with?"

"They're not wacky. They're just super-slutty!"

"I think you're one wacky slut."

"Thanks! But you're the one who's been fucked a million times by T-69. So who's really the biggest slut here?"

"Hey! That's only because you left me alone with it for so long."

"And did you refuse any of the fuckings?"

"Um, no."

"Did you love all the fuckings?"

"Um, yes."

"Then you're the biggest slut!"

Remy sighed. "Okay, I'm the biggest slut. But do you really want to be a slut out in public?"

Sam tapped her lips. "Hmm, good point. T-69, maybe we should hold off on that."

"Negative. Move your sexy assess immediately." It

grabbed each of their posteriors and marched them toward the door.

"Ack!" Sam yelped. "I think I've lost control of my creation."

"No kidding!" Remy agreed. "And it means we're about to become public whores!"

# Chapter 13

The sun shone brightly off Remy's naked body as T-69 ushered Sam and her into the parking lot.

She tried to head back inside, but the robot had a vice grip on her ass.

"Are you trying to retreat back into the lab?" it asked.

"Yes!" Remy replied. "We're totally naked!"

"Of course. You are both sluts."

"I really think I'm more of an indoor slut."

"I don't know," Sam said. "I don't see any tan lines on that gorgeous body."

Remy blushed as she scanned her nude form. Her half-Mexican heritage had blessed her with skin that turned a pleasing golden brown in the sun. And it was true she had no tan lines. "Um, well, that's because I sunbathe in the nude in my backyard when my parents aren't home. But no one else can see me."

Sam's eyes lit up. "Ooh, sexy! Since I have your address

from the forms you filled out, I can reposition satellites to peep on you the next time you sunbathe."

"What?! Can you really do that? You're a sexy evil genius!" Remy was more impressed with Sam's geeky skills than worried about the scientist peeping on her. In fact, it'd be pretty hot if Sam did ogle her naked body with satellite imagery.

"No," Sam replied. "Well, maybe, but I'd have to do some seriously illegal hacking. It might be worth it though." She licked her lips as she once again took in Remy's nudeness.

That made the young co-ed warm between her legs. "Please spy on me with all your naughty technology! I'll finger myself in my backyard if I know you're watching."

"Aha! So you are an outdoor slut!"

"Only when sexy girls are watching."

"I'm watching now. Aren't I a sexy girl?"

"Soooo sexy!"

"Then let's be outdoor sluts together!"

Remy giggled. The kinky doc's enthusiasm for slutty shenanigans was contagious.

She glanced around. The homeless man from before had apparently moved on, and no one else was in sight. If she was going to be fucked by a robot out in the open, this was the time to do it.

She looked up at her robot master. "Okay, T-69, please make us public whores."

"That is what I am programmed to do." It bent Remy over the hood of her jeep, the magnetic rings around her wrists sticking to the metal, so she couldn't move her hands.

"Y... you're going to fuck me on my jeep?"

"Of course."

"O... okay." Remy had certainly had sex inside vehicles before, but never bent over one. T-69 really knew how to push her kinky buttons.

"Great idea, T-69!" Sam commented. "Her ass looks scrumptious bent over like that."

"Um, can you note on the feedback form at the end of this that I have a scrumptious ass?" Remy asked. It wasn't every day a sexy lady described her tush in such flattering terms.

"Sure! I'll write stuff about your butt, pussy, and tits. And about how much of a whore you are!"

"Um, I don't know if everyone needs to know that."

"Well, they'll find out soon enough if T-69 keeps fucking you in public."

"Oh, I guess that's true. Wait, how many other public places are you taking us to?"

The robot rubbed her butt. "I have not decided. It depends on how submissive you are during this first outing."

Remy shivered. She wasn't sure if being more or less submissive would lead to more or less public whoring, but she had a feeling she wasn't going to have much of a choice. Once T-69 started fucking her, she couldn't resist fully submitting to it.

"I think you should fuck her now, T-69," Sam encouraged.

"Affirmative, Doctor. But I will fuck both of you." He effortlessly tossed her on top of Remy, her wrist magnets sticking to the younger slut's. T-69 had made sure to attach the metal bracelets around Sam's wrists and ankles before marching them outside. The robot wanted to have full control over their limbs as well as their pussies and asses.

Sam's cute breasts rubbed against Remy's back and her even cuter pussy against Remy's ass. She was glad she wouldn't be the only one fucked on her car. But she still was going to tease Sam about it. "Haha, you're getting fucked too, you horny doc!"

"Well, at least I have the world's greatest ass to grind

against," she replied.

Remy blushed. "World's greatest ass? Oh, stop."

"It's the greatest ass I've ever seen. I want to use it as a pillow at night and then slap it all day long!"

Remy blushed even more. "Um, that can probably be arranged." Remy's butt was so full and juicy that more than one former lover had enjoyed resting their heads on it. Maybe she should rent her booty out at the beach for people to lay on while they sunbathed. She could make some good money and get a nice tan. Except she'd probably get a weird head-shaped tan line on her ass. So maybe that wouldn't work after all. But she could still let Sam sleep on her butt.

"Great! I'm obsessed with your ass."

"I love people who are obsessed with my ass!" Remy cheered.

"And I enjoy sluts who know their place," T-69 told them as it shoved four cocks into their pussies and asses.

"Holy robot cocks!!!" Remy screamed.

"You said it, Robin!!" Sam replied. Remy knew Sam was her kind of girl. Besides for loving robot dick, the hot doc obviously loved superheroes and other geeky stuff. Her reference of Robin from the 1960s Batman TV show was spot on. Remy's parents made sure to bring her up on all the classic sci-fi, fantasy, and superhero movies and shows. That was parenting done right, at least in her book. They had not taught her to be a sci-fi slut, however. She was learning that all on her own. And probably wouldn't share that with her parents. They were cool, but she wasn't sure if any parent wanted to learn their daughter had been ravaged by five aliens and a sex robot. Some things were better left unshared. Though if T-69 kept fucking her this hard, she'd be sharing her throaty screams with the whole world.

The robot rammed both her holes, and did the same to Sam's just above her.

"F… fuuuuccccckkk, T-69," Remy moaned. "People are going to hear us if you keep fucking us so hard." No one had seemed to notice them so far. But there was an area of the strip mall at the other end of the parking lot that was occupied, so it was only a matter of time.

"Y… yeah," Sam echoed. "I can't stop moaning and shrieking."

"Does that mean you are enjoying my large cocks?"

"I sure am!" Sam told it.

"I love them even more!" Remy screamed, for some reason

wanting to prove she was the bigger slut.

"Hey, it's not a competition."

"It could be a competition."

"But I built T-69."

"Yeah, but I was his first slut."

"Cease your bickering. I will ensure each of you are equal in how slutty you become."

Remy smiled through her moans. "Aw, thanks T-69!" Wait, was she thanking the robot for making her a huge whore? Well, why not? She appreciated his sense of fairness: he wasn't going to choose a favorite among his human sluts. T-69 was her kind of robot!

"We promise we'll behave!" Sam wailed, her wet pussy rubbing back and forth across Remy's ass. The doc's juices spilled down Remy's ass crack, making the younger woman feel even sluttier.

"Sam's cumming all over my ass!" she announced, figuring T-69 would want to know that key information.

"That is excellent. She should cover your entire buttocks in her nectar."

"I sure will!" Sam screamed, shooting out even more of her potent punch.

Remy was absolutely loving being fucked with Sam. But she knew they were getting way too loud. "T… T-69, we can't control our screams. Can you please bring us inside?"

"I have a better solution." It snatched two small cloths from a compartment inside its body and stuffed them in Remy and Sam's mouths, tying them behind their heads.

"Mmmrphhh!" Remy moaned. She had never been gagged before, but it was kind of hot. And it was muffling her screams to a decibel that wouldn't be overheard.

The jeep shook back and forth as the two gagged women were fucked out of their minds.

Remy had never felt so exposed or so submissive. She was at the mercy of her robot lover, knowing there was a chance of someone coming by at any moment.

She gazed at the people exiting the stores on the other side of the parking lot. She could barely make them out, but she pretended some of them had binoculars and were watching her and Sam get their pussies and asses owned.

"I will now cum inside all four of your holes," T-69 informed them. "You will take it like good human sluts."

Remy and Sam moaned their assent through their gags. They were very ready to be filled with robot semen.

Both women squealed as T-69 unloaded its fake cum into them. Sam wiggled around on top of Remy, her first experience with robot jizz driving her wild.

Remy was squirming around just as much. Her pussy rubbed against the hood, making her have her own orgasm. She flooded the metal, her writhing body smearing it all over. Guess she didn't have to get a car wash now. If T-69 kept fucking them out here, she and Sam would be able to clean her entire jeep. Though she hoped any seepage wouldn't mess up the engine. Well, it could take rain showers, so surely it could take cum showers too.

The girls screamed and shrieked as T-69 pumped round after round into them.

The robot finally pulled out, inordinate amounts of its cum leaking out of their pussies and assess. The cum from Sam's holes poured across Remy's ass, making her posterior very sticky.

T-69 removed their gags, letting them pant and moan and cum some more. "How do you feel?" it asked.

"S... so full of your cum!" Remy gasped.

"I've never felt so slutty in my life!" Sam confessed.

"Excellent. I have fulfilled my programming. Now I must

go recharge." It rotated on its robot legs and headed for the entrance.

"Wait!" Remy said. "We're still stuck to the hood."

"Affirmative." It continued toward the door.

"Aren't you going to untie us?" Sam asked.

"Negative." Without further explanation, it entered the lab and shut the door behind it.

Remy trembled beneath Sam. They were tied to the hood, naked, with cum dripping from their pussies and asses. And those pussies and assess were in prime position for anyone to fuck. "Um, Sam, is your robot supposed to do that?"

"Not really. I think it's taking my programming too literally."

"But you told it to make all women sluts."

"Well, it sounded like a good idea at the time."

Remy rolled her eyes. Sexy scientists were very kooky. "What are we going to do? We're stuck out here and completely helpless."

"Yeah, pretty hot, huh?"

"Hot?! We're going to become the town fuck toys!"

"Damn, it's even hotter when you put it like that. And don't pretend you're not getting turned on. I can tell you just came."

Remy blushed. "H… how did you know?"

"Your hips do a little shimmy every time you climax. It's very cute."

"Oh. Thanks! I've been shimmying a lot today."

"I bet!"

"But, seriously, what should we do?"

"Nothing. Just wait until someone comes along to help. Or even better, someone with a big cock to fuck us!"

Remy shimmied again. If they were discovered, would people line up to take turns ramming their helpless holes? Would they be filled with every sample of semen the residents had to offer?

Oh boy, Remy was seriously considering becoming a public fuck toy.

# Chapter 14

Remy wiggled on the hood of her jeep as Sam came all over her ass.

"Sam! You're cumming on my butt."

"That's because you're rubbing your hot ass against my pussy."

"I am? Oops, sorry, I didn't know I was doing it."

"Don't apologize. Do it more!"

'Okay!" Remy wiggled as much as she could within her magnetic bonds, stimulating Sam's cute pussy so much, Remy's ass crack was flooded with the scientist's tasty juices. "Oh my God, you're such a good cummer!"

"I have a lot of practice. I masturbate all the time at home, work, the supermarket, pretty much everywhere."

"The supermarket?! Where can you do it in there?"

"The frozen foods section. It makes my nipples nice and hard!"

Remy giggled. Then trembled as she pictured Sam with

her shirt raised above her breasts, nipples all perky, hand down her shorts as she played with herself. "Can you take me shopping with you next time?"

"Sure! I'll finger you really hard."

Remy trembled even more. She really wanted the hot doc to fuck her in a supermarket, where everyone could watch and see what a slut she was. Yikes! She was really becoming quite the exhibitionist. It had to be those horny aliens and equally horny robot. They were turning her into a nymphomaniac. Thank goodness she had met them!

The roar of a pickup truck broke her out of her sexy reverie.

"Ack!" Remy wailed. "Someone's coming."

"Great!" Sam replied. "We can get fucked again."

"How do you know they'll want to fuck us?"

"We're two sexy, naked girls tied to the hood of a car. Who wouldn't want to fuck us?"

"Oh. Good point." Remy tingled at the thought of a stranger plowing her holes while she was helpless. And then maybe he could call his friends and invite them to fuck her while she was still helpless. Goodness, she was having very illicit fantasies ever since her encounter with the aliens. Those well-endowed extraterrestrials could probably bring peace to Earth if they made everyone horny sluts.

The truck pulled up next to Remy's jeep. A handyman hopped out. He wore faded work jeans and an open vest that reveled his hairy, tanned, muscular chest. He had a mustache and short dark beard and was ruggedly handsome.

He placed his tool belt on the hood of his truck and stared in surprise at the naked, bound women.

"Oh, hi!" Sam greeted him cheerfully. "I forgot you were coming today."

"Are you… Dr. Shen?" he asked, still trying to figure out what was going on.

"Yup! And this is my assistant, Remy."

"Um, hello." Rem wiggled her fingers in a wave, beyond mortified to be meeting someone while she was naked and tied up. And since when did she become Sam's assistant? Well, she was assisting her with seeing how much T-69 could turn her into a raging sex maniac. So she supposed the moniker fit.

"Is this a bad time?" he asked. He was obviously trying to be polite, but his eyes roamed both women's wet, nude bodies. And the bulge in his tight jeans grew until it threatened to burst the fabric. Remy couldn't take her eyes off it. He had quite the beast. A beast she desperately wanted in her pussy.

"No, it's a great time!" Sam replied.

"So, you still want work done on your building?"

"No, we want work done on our slutholes! Please fuck us! Um, if that's okay with you, Assistant Remy?"

Remy trembled beneath her. It was more than okay with her. "Yes, I need lots of work done on my pussy and ass, Dr. Shen!" She groaned as soon as she said it. It sounded like her naughty holes were in a state of disrepair and needed fixing. That might not be the biggest turn-on to a hunky handyman. "Oh, I mean, there's nothing wrong with my pussy and ass. They're both really firm and tight. I just really want your cock inside them. That is, if you don't mind fucking us, Mr. Hunky Handyman. And, um, I'll think I'll shut up now." Remy groaned again, wishing she hadn't just word vomited all over the place.

Sam giggled and came all over Remy's ass. "My assistant is kind of dorky, but she has the tightest pussy and ass you'll ever fuck. That's why I keep her around."

Now it was Remy who was cumming. She liked hearing

she had the tightest pussy and ass in town. But was that really why Sam chose her? Actually, it made sense. Remy was here to let T-69 fuck her in whatever way it wanted, so a juicy pussy and ass were important requirements. And Sam wasn't wrong about Remy being dorky. She loved all things geeky and was quite proud of that. Though she knew Sam was going to tease her mercilessly about her awkwardness trying to talk to the handyman. Remy was much better with aliens and robots. Talking to hunky guys was hard.

Sam's words had the desired effect. The beefy guy's penis pulsated in his jeans. Remy could clearly see it throbbing, begging to be let loose on the two bound sluts.

He tore off his vest and strode toward them. "I'll make sure you're satisfied with my job performance."

Remy and Sam both came again. They were both crazy wet and crazy ready to be fucked.

He undid his belt and unbuttoned his pants.

Remy's eyes were locked on his crotch as he slowly unzipped, revealing the huge bulge within his tight boxer briefs.

"Please show us your penis!" Remy wailed, then immediately gasped, surprised at her forthrightness. "Um, I mean, if you don't mind."

"My assistant is very horny," Sam giggled.

The man smiled and pulled down his pants and underwear. His cock sprang loose, its massiveness bobbing before them.

"Oh wow," Sam said.

"Sooooo big," Remy marveled.

His cock quivered, enjoying the girls' compliments. He approached them, running his strong hands along their legs and thighs. "Who should I start with?"

"Me!" they both shouted.

"I'm the one who called him," Sam pointed out.

"But I'm hornier!" Remy replied. She wasn't sure if that was true. The sexy doc was a very horny woman too. But Remy had been fucked so much by T-69, she couldn't imagine anyone being more sex-obsessed than her right now.

"Are not!"

"Are too!" Remy realized they were being childish, and the handyman probably would happily fuck both of them. But she really wanted to feel his cock right this instant. Her pussy was throbbing, begging her to fill it with something, ideally a nice meaty penis.

He spanked both of them.

"Ow!" Remy yelped.

"Eek!" Sam whimpered.

"Ladies, please stop bickering. I will make sure you are both properly fucked."

"Thank you!" Sam replied.

"We're sorry," Remy added. "Can you please teach us to be proper sluts?"

He spanked them again. "Gladly." His cock slapped against Sam's ass. Remy was jealous she wasn't the one on top. She wanted his big dick spanking her. But her jealously quickly evaporated when he inserted two fingers in her pussy.

"Ohhhhh fuck!" she moaned. Sam made similar noises, telling Remy she was getting the dual-finger treatment too.

The hunky handyman probed deeply into Remy's tightness. His fingers were rough and calloused, which allowed them to stimulate Remy's insides even more than usual.

"Fu… fuck, you're so strong," she told him between gasps.

"Pound us harder!" Sam begged.

He did, slamming his fingers into their drenched holes. Remy realized their moans were getting so loud they were in danger of alerting everyone in the vicinity again. And they didn't have the gags T-69 had so handily provided. So she pressed her mouth against the hood, using it to muffle her screams. Sam buried her face in Remy's neck, using a similar technique to mask her erotic cries.

Their inability to stifle their moans made the handyman pound them even harder. So hard they squirted all over his fingers and their own bodies. They shook and trembled and told him they were his sluts.

Now that he knew they were his sluts, he decided they deserved his big cock. He pressed it against Remy's lips.

She gasped, beyond excited that he had chosen her to be the first to receive his massive gift. Her pussy parted eagerly for him, and he entered her.

"Ohhhh fuuuuuccccckkkkk!" He was so big, and he felt so good.

"Aww," Sam complained. "No fair, you get his juicy cock first."

Their handsome lover stuck his finger in Sam's ass.

"Holy shit!!" the sexy scientist squealed. "Never mind, please fuck my butt!"

Remy smiled through her moans. She was glad Sam was

getting a good fucking along with her. And boy was she getting a good fucking. The handyman slammed his hips against her, thrusting fully into her every time. Remy was worried after aliens and robots, humans might not do it for her. But this guy was proving that theory wrong. He really knew how to use his dick.

"Do you two always hang around naked outside, waiting to be fucked?" he asked between grunts and groans.

"Yes! All the time!" Sam replied, wiggling her stuffed butt on top of Remy.

"Sam, don't lie!" Remy admonished. "Th… this is actually our first time."

"Speak for yourself, sister."

Remy moaned especially hard, wondering how many times Sam tied herself up in public and waited for sexy men and women to fuck her.

"And don't pretend you don't fantasize about being ravished when you sunbathe nude in your backyard," Sam continued.

Remy shivered. How did Sam know that's what she imagined when she was being naughty at home? That's why Remy always wound up masturbating when she was soaking in the rays in her backyard. Though she had to keep her moans down so the neighbors didn't know how slutty she was. "Sam! You're not supposed to tell everyone that."

"I enjoy hearing it," their current lover said, ramming her even harder.

"Oh, o… okay!" Remy moaned. If it meant he'd fuck her even harder, she'd confess any slutty thing he wanted.

"Would you like me to come into your backyard and fuck you while you sunbathe?" he asked.

"Oh God, yes! I'll sunbathe every day so you can come and fuck me!" Remy pictured her nude body gleaming in the sun, his hunky form casting a shadow across her, then pressing his hard body against her and ravaging her to his heart's content. Fuck, that was so hot! "But, um, can you come when my parents aren't there?" Oh crap, Remy realized she was volunteering more information than necessary. It probably wasn't that sexy to tell him she could only have sex when her parents weren't home. "Oh, I mean, I just live with them because I'm still in college. I'll get my own place after that and you can come fuck me as much as you want. Unless it's an apartment and I don't have a backyard. That might make sunbathing hard. But I'll still happily get naked for you and let you fuck me wherever you want."

Sam giggled uncontrollably, spilling her naughty sauce across Remy's ass.

Remy blushed. "Oops, I'm doing it again, aren't I?" Why did she keep blurting out all this unnecessary info?

"Yes, but it's very cute," Sam told her.

"Okay, I'll be quiet, and, um, just let you fuck us super-hard."

"Don't be too quiet," the man told them. "I love haring you moan and whimper for me."

Remy and Sam moaned and whimpered for him.

He enjoyed it so much that he came hard. He pulled out just before he did, spraying his seed across the asses of his two sluts.

"Oh my goodness, you're cumming so much!" Sam remarked.

"I'm so sticky!" Remy added.

"You'll be a lot stickier before long," he told them. "But first..."

He got on his knees and licked their pussies, showing he knew how to use his mouth as well as his cock. He made them both squirt and lapped them up, which is what any true gentleman did. Remy appreciated that he was both strong and sweet. Her kind of guy!

That gave his penis time to recover, and he gave Sam's pussy the fucking it had so patiently been waiting for. Remy wasn't left out: he shoved his finger in her super-tight ass.

Remy tensed, then relaxed, letting him probe as far in as he wanted. She had come to relish anal, loving how it felt to have her ass explored by humans, robots, and aliens.

When he finished with them, they were spent, sticky, and feeling super-slutty.

"Should I untie you or leave you like this?" he asked, rubbing their butts gently.

"You can leave us like this," the kooky doc replied.

"Sam!"

"Okay, okay, I guess you better untie us."

He did, and helped steady them as they got to their feet.

"Do you still want me to take a look at your roof?" he asked.

"Oh, sure," Sam answered. "You're obviously really good with your hands."

He grinned and returned to his truck to gather equipment.

"Um, can we go inside now?" Remy asked.

"I thought you liked being a public slut."

"Well, it is kind of fun. But I think maybe I should be an indoor slut for the rest of the day."

"Okay! I like you slutty inside or out."

Remy giggled. This was one weird scientist.

They re-entered the building and poked their heads inside the main room. T-69 stood motionless, evidently still recharging. Remy understood why it would need to. The robot had really worked over Remy and Sam's slutty bodies. They had done a good job draining its batteries.

"We need to sneak up and deactivate it," Sam whispered.

"We're not going to let it fuck us a bunch more?" Remy asked, a little disappointed.

"Ooh, you little robot slut."

"I am not. Um, okay, maybe I am. But that's because you left me with T-69 all day."

"Oh yeah, sorry about that."

"Don't be sorry. It was amazing!"

"Great! But I need to reprogram it or it's going to turn us into its sex slaves forever."

Remy nodded. While the thought of that was enticing, she had a life she had to get back to. Being a robot sex toy from time to time was fine, but not every hour of every day. "How do we deactivate it?"

"I need to access a panel on its upper back."

"Okay, let's go."

She and Sam crept across the room, looking rather ridiculous being naked and with cum dripping off them.

Remy kept her gaze locked on the robot, worried that it might spring to life at any moment. Well, half-worried, half-excited. A big part of her wanted T-69 to continue showing her what a good robot slut she was.

Sam moved a chair behind her creation and climbed onto it, so she could reach its upper back.

Remy stood before T-69, watching it carefully. She hoped Sam could reprogram it so it would still treat them like sluts but not want to turn every woman in the world into a whore. That might be a little extreme.

Sam gingerly touched the plate on its back.

And that's when T-69's eyes opened and glowed brightly.

Those eyes stared right at Remy.

She gulped. Oh fuck.

# Chapter 15

"Dr. Shen, what are you doing?" T-69 asked.

Sam paused, her fingers on the robot's neck panel. "Oh, just doing some routine maintenance. Gotta make sure you're in tip top shape to fuck us."

"Yes. That is my mission. But I'm registering your voice at a higher pitch than usual, which would indicate you are telling a falsehood."

"What?!!" Sam replied at an even higher pitch. "Th… that's ridiculous. I always tell the truth."

"Dr. Shen, I will have to punish you with many spankings for your subterfuge."

Remy fidgeted in front of the robot. She had to do something quick before T-69 snatched Sam and fucked her until she agreed to be its sex slave forever. "T-69, I need to suck your dick!" she cried.

The robot turned its attention to her.

"I was going through withdrawal while you were

recharging," she continued. "I need your cock so bad. I need you to show me what a good robot slut I am. Please turn me into your sex slave!" Remy hoped the sex machine wouldn't be able to resist her desperate pleas for domination. And she wasn't even acting: she loved how it fucked her holes and made her its whore.

"I am glad you know your place, Remy the Slut," he told her. "I will now fuck you vigorously."

Remy tingled. "Yes! Please fuck me! I'm Remy the Slut and I deserve to be a sex toy!" She was really enjoying this over-the-top slutty begging. She hoped her sexy distracting would give Sam the time she needed to modify the robot's programming.

T-69 shoved Remy to her knees and squatted, one of its huge prosthetic cocks springing forth from a compartment between its legs.

The technological marvel grabbed Remy's head and plunged her mouth onto its dick.

"Mrmph!!" Remy gasped, not realizing the robot was going to make her deep throat its cock so quickly. But she did tell it she wanted to be the ultimate robot slut. So it only made sense for her mouth to be its fuck toy.

It thrust her mouth back and forth, nearly making Remy gag. Even though its cock was artificial, it felt very real. And tasted even better than a human dick. Remy found herself eager to suck the robot off.

"You have an excellent mouth to fuck," T-69 told her.

Remy gave it a thumbs-up, happy to get its praise. She didn't know how Sam was making out with the panel, but she hoped her nutty scientist friend didn't reprogram her lover too quickly. She wanted one last huge fucking before Sam turned T-69 off.

"I will now cum in your mouth," her metallic master informed her.

Remy moaned her assent, and was soon swallowing a boatload of yummy robot cum. She made sure to swallow it all to make T-69 happy. She knew it didn't like it when she let any of its seed go to waste.

She gasped as it removed her mouth from its cock, gazing up at him with slutty eyes. Sam was still tinkering behind T-69, so Remy needed to keep distracting the sex-obsessed invention. Lucky her!

"Please fuck my pussy and ass!" she begged it.

"Affirmative." It lifted her off the floor and deposited her two holes on two juicy cocks, a huge one for her pussy and a slightly smaller one for her ass.

"Holy robot cocks!!" she wailed, both slut holes squeezing the delicious dicks, never wanting to let go.

She tried to wrap her legs around T-69's bulk. Restraints sprung from its sides, pinning her legs to its hips. Other bindings wrapped around her wrists and back, holding her tightly to its chest.

"Oh God, I'm completely helpless!" She wiggled around, barely able to move.

"Affirmative. Now I may fuck you like the sexy human whore you are."

Remy tingled again. Sexy human whore? Geez, T-69 was getting dirtier and dirtier with its names for her. But she liked that it thought she was sexy. And she didn't mind being its whore one bit.

Its dual cocks went into action, jackhammering both her holes and making her scream in pleasure.

"Ohhhh my fucking Godddddddd!! I'm such a robot slut!!!"

"You are an excellent submissive human."

"Th… thank you!"

Sam stared from behind T-69's shoulder, watching in awe

at the slutty faces Remy was making. Remy knew she should probably nudge Sam to get back to work, but she was deliriously happy with how T-69 was fucking her. He was ramming her so hard, all she could think about was how she wanted to be its sex slave, its fuck toy, its robot cum dump.

"Fuck, fuck, fuck, I'm such a slut!!"

"Affirmative," it agreed.

"I need your cum inside me so bad!" she begged.

"I will fill both your pussy and ass until you are overflowing."

"Yes!! Please flood me with your delicious robot juices!" Remy had completely lost all control. She didn't care what Sam was doing. She just needed to feel T-69's thick fluid coursing into her, letting her know she was its property and could fuck her as it saw fit.

"I am cumming," it said in its unenthusiastic robot voice. Remy would have giggled at how silly that orgasmic revelation sounded, but she was too busy squirming under the onslaught of robot cum flowing into her.

"Ohhh fuck, it's so much!!" She knew she couldn't contain it all, and it was soon squirting out of both her pussy and ass.

And then she was squirting her own juices. T-69 vibrated

her clit and gave her one orgasm after another. She screamed and moaned and knew she wanted to be a robot slut until the end of time.

But her robot slut time was short-lived. T-69 shut down with a whine, its cocks coming to a rest fully inside her.

"Got it!" Sam cried, glancing down at Remy.

"Ohhhhhhh!" Remy squealed. She was still shaking from her orgasms and still had a ridiculous amount of T-69's cum inside her, though it was slowly seeping out of both her slut holes.

"Are you okay?" Sam asked.

"Y… yeah. I'm just stuck on its cocks and have so much cum in me."

"Oh, right. Hang on." Sam fiddled with the back panel.

The restraints released. The cocks retracted. And Remy fell to the floor with a thud.

"Ow," she groaned, rolling onto her side to let the sticky robot cum flow out of her.

Sam hopped down and knelt beside her. "Wow, T-69 really filled you."

"Uh… uh huh." Remy felt very slutty with Sam watching the thick white liquid pour from her pussy and ass. But she didn't mind the sexy scientist seeing her in such a submissive state.

Sam rubbed Remy's thigh. "You were an amazing slutty distraction."

"Th… thanks. I, um, kinda got lost in the moment."

"Oh, I could tell. You really wanted to be its fuck toy forever."

"No, I didn't!"

Sam pinched her. "Stop fibbing, you little slut."

Remy blushed as more cum oozed out of her. "Well, maybe. It's really good at dominating girls."

"Yup. I'm an excellent mad scientist."

Remy laughed. "You sure are. But you're a sexy one, so it's okay."

Now Sam was blushing. "R… really?"

"Yes, you're super-hot, you nutty genius."

Sam beamed. "Thanks! You're the best assistant ever!"

"Wait, I thought I was just here to be a test subject. When did I become your assistant?"

"When we both became robot sluts together."

Remy nodded. "Oh, okay, that makes sense."

Sam helped Remy sit up and held her tightly. Remy

snuggled into Sam and eked out the rest of T-69's cum.

"I'll be your assistant, but only if you take me out on a date," she told the older scientist.

Sam gasped. "You want to go out with me?"

"Yeah, you're fun and sexy, and who else can I talk to about being fucked by a robot?"

Sam laughed. "Good point. Okay, it's a date! I'll take you somewhere really nice to make up for all the shenanigans I put you through."

Remy kissed her cheek. "That's okay, I like sexy shenanigans. You should hear about how I got fucked by a bunch of aliens."

"What?!!!" Sam's mouth dropped open like she had just won the Sexiest Scientist of the Year award. Which Remy thought should totally be a real thing.

"I'll tell you all about it on our date." Remy snuggled in closer, glad she had someone she could share her illicit exploits with.

She had a feeling there would be a lot more of those exploits in the future.

It was good to be an alien and robot slut!

**Check Out More Episodes of Remy and the Sex Monsters on Kindle Vella**

Remy and the Sex Monsters in an ongoing Kindle Vella series with new episodes released weekly. This volume includes Episodes 1-15 of the series, but there are many more to check out. Read more of Remy's sexy, submissive adventures on the Kindle Vella page!

**Get Fully Nude and Erotic Covers and Pics!**

You can get Nude and Sex Covers of this and other books as well as almost one hundred naked/erotic pictures of my characters on my Riley Rose Erotica Patreon Page. Just go to Patreon.com/RileyRoseErotica to check them out!

**Check Out More of My Fun and Sexy Books**

**Sexy Time Cop: Cowgirl and Pirate Sluts**

Riley Shu is a Time Cop, traveling to amazing periods in the past to stop criminals from latering the timeline. And having sex with some of the hottest men and women in history! She has to save Doc Holliday from a future felon and gets in some kinky cowgirl fun along the way. Then it's off to the Golden Age of Piracy for some submissive shenanigans with the most famous female pirate of all time: Anne Bonny!

**Sex with My Robot Car**

Mara Keoni is a sexy Navajo special agent of the Independent Justice Foundation. But she never expected to be paired with KATT, an incredibly advanced female AI inside a sports car. Not only is KATT very eager to help Mara on her missions, but she's also eager to pleasure Mara in every way possible with her many "enhancements." Will Mara succumb to her curiosity and find out exactly what KATT can do to her? Find out in Sex with My Robot Car!

**Cybernetic Sex: Virtual Bondage**

Aiya Arakawa has the most powerful and sexiest cybernetic body on the planet. She uses it to complete dangerous missions for Section 8, a secret branch of the Japanese government. And to have lots of amazing sex with humans, androids, and fellow cybernetics. When she gets an upgrade that kicks her pleasure receptors into overdrive, will she be able to handle the overload of pleasure at the hands of enemy AIs, sexy thieves, and android courtesans?

**Tantalizing Tentacles Series**

Kione Ali is an adventurous treasure hunter, always looking to find the next big score. When she gets a clue to Blackbeard's treasure in Barbados, she can't pass up the opportunity to score the notorious pirate's booty. But she never expected to find a tentacle creature with the treasure, one that wants to pleasure Kione in every way possible and tie her up like the submissive sex object she is. Will Kione give in to her kinky curiosity to have tentacle sex? Will she let it explore every inch of her caverns? Find out in this sexy, sensual, tentacle adventure!

Visit RileyRoseErotica.com to get a Free eBook and learn more about my books and the Decadent Fantasy Universe!

E-mail: Riley@RileyRoseErotica.com

Facebook: RileyRoseErotica
Twitter: @RileyRoserotica
Instagram: @RileyRoseErotica

## About the Author

Riley Rose writes comedic, sexy stories featuring fun-loving female protagonists who love taking their clothes off. Discover sexy sci-fi, fantasy, and action/adventure worlds in over forty books and Kindle Vella stories, featuring naughty witches, frisky fairy tale characters, sex-obsessed robots, and titillating tentacles. You'll find fun, friendship, and a ton of submissive sex in Riley's books. Join the sexy shenanigans! Find out more at RileyRoseErotica.com.